A Spectacular Event

An Oak Harbor Series

Kimberly Thomas

Prologue

One month ago

"You should try the steak, dear, it's deliciously decadent. I had the chef prepare it, especially for you. I want your honest opinion."

Rory smiled politely at the woman seated at the far end of the table. Her deep blue eyes stared back at her, assessing. She returned her attention to the dish before her. She'd already eaten most of the meager portion of baked potato, broccoli, and carrots but skirted around the slab of steak in the center of the plate. She gingerly speared the meat with her fork and used her knife to slice off a small piece. Blood oozed from the middle of the dark red meat, causing her to cringe internally as she brought it to her mouth.

"It is good, yes?"

Surprisingly the steak was tender, and she could taste the smoky charcoal aroma as the juices connected with her tongue, but then there was a metallic taste of blood that triggered her gag reflexes. She swallowed, then reached for her champagne flute to wash away the taste.

"It is...nice," she managed to turn and reply. The woman gave her a triumphant smile before turning her attention back to her plate. She delicately sliced off a piece of her stake and placed it in her mouth to chew demurely.

Rory felt something brush against her ankle. She looked across the table to see her fiancé's concerned blue eyes staring back at her. She fought to lift the corners of her mouth into a reassuring smile.

"How are the wedding plans coming along, dear?"

Rory returned her attention to her mother-in-law, already staring back at her. She paused before answering the question, already knowing that there was a strong possibility that her response would possibly unsettle the woman.

"There are a few changes, but it's still on track. I have...I mean," she paused to look over at James. He smiled back encouragingly. "We have decided to have the wedding in Oak Harbor."

Lenora's eyes widened in surprise before something dark flashed in their blue depths. The woman managed to school her expression as she asked, "When did you make this decision?" Her focus turned to her son.

"Four days ago," James replied before adding, "We both decided it was the best option. It will allow Rory's family to be more involved in the wedding and give us a chance to get to know them better." He looked over at his fiancé with an affectionate smile which Rory returned, grateful for his explanation.

"But you already decided to have the wedding at our church. Father Jeremiah has already marked the date on his calendar, and what about your booking at Le Meridien for the reception?" Lenora pressed.

"We've already withdrawn our appointment for Le Meridien. There wasn't a penalty fee because the wedding was months away." This time it was Rory who spoke up.

"Father Jeremiah will understand, Mom," James added.

"And our guests, our family; what do I tell them?" Lenora persisted, looking pointedly at her son.

"We haven't sent out the invitations yet, so it's fine," he responded.

"But, but—"

"Mom, it's fine," James spoke with a smile of reassurance.

Lenora's eyes went to the other end of the table where her husband sat the entire time, focused on finishing his meal and unbothered by the conversation. As if sensing his wife's eyes on him, Richard looked up, quirking a brow. Lenora's lips spread into a grim line, and she averted her eyes to her plate, her eyebrows furrowed as she blinked rapidly. When she looked up again, a smile was on her lips, but Rory could see that it was a strained one.

"Very well then, Oak Harbor it is," she said lightly. "You must let me help you plan for the wedding, dear. It's the least I can do, seeing as the wedding will no longer be in San Fran." Her eyes flashed with determination as she stared at Rory.

"Um...our wedding planner Jennifer already has everything under control. I'm not sure how much input you'll get, Lenora," Rory answered carefully.

"I understand, but I want to do this for you and my son. You're about to become a part of our family now, and I've always imagined that whomever James marries, I would help to plan the wedding. It's the least I can do." The intonation in her voice suggested that if Rory refused, it would be a great disappointment on her end.

"Okay. I'll talk to Jennifer and let her know you will be offering your input," Rory conceded.

"Good," Lenora returned with a self-satisfied smirk.

Rory was sure she'd just lost a great battle, and a sinking

feeling settled in her chest. "Please excuse me." She placed her napkin on her chair as she stood.

James stood as well, the look of concern etched across his face. "Are you alright?" he asked.

"I am," Rory replied, a tiny smile of reassurance on her lips. "I just need to..."

She didn't finish the sentence. James nodded in understanding. Stepping away from the table, she headed for the hallway. Her low heels clicked against the marble floor and echoed throughout the cavernous open space as she made her way toward the powder room. The room was toward the end of the long hallway, which felt more like a runway rather than just the entryway for the numerous rooms on the first floor of the mansion.

Rory slipped into the room, and the door closed behind her with a soft click. She walked over to the porcelain sink. Flattening her palms against the cold, hard surface, she bowed her head, eyes cast down in exhaustion. The meeting with her in-laws felt more stressful than normal.

Staring at her reflection in the gilded mirror in front of her, she winced at the evident fatigue on her face. She placed her hands together, forming a cup before putting them under the tap. It came on automatically, and the water rushed out to fill up the indentation of her joined palms. Rory splashed the water against her face welcoming the coolness on her cheeks. Hopefully, it would help the color return in them.

"Okay, Rory, you can do this. Just a few more hours, then you get to go home and hopefully enjoy that tub of ice cream you've been ignoring for the past couple of weeks."

She sighed miserably. Who was she kidding? This evening was bound to get more unbearable the longer she and James stayed. She was sure Lenora was only bidding her time before she started picking on her about her appearance, her choice of occupation and anything else that she was sure would get to Rory.

It had been like this ever since she and James started dating. When she first met James' parents, she immediately sensed the disappointment that oozed off them in waves, Lenora especially. She had been incredibly catty and had brought Rory to the brink of tears. It had made her reconsider dating James.

Lenora made it a point of reference to mention that they, in fact, were from two different backgrounds. He was born to generational wealth and would always be wealthy, while she had been born to a mother who raised her single-handedly, who struggled hard to make a life for the both of them. The stark difference had been made even more abundantly clear on her first visit to the Davis' mansion.

The degree of opulence in the sprawling three-story house that she came to understand sat on its own thirty-two acres of land and boasted a garden that could rival that of the Queen of England's and littered with other amenities such as swimming pools and tennis courts had intimidated her. She'd been set on breaking up with James, but he had convinced her that he was in this for the long haul and would get his parents to understand. That was the first time he'd said, "I love you." His revelation had melted her heart, and she'd also decided to fight for their relationship. Whatever James said to his parents, Lenora had become more welcoming, but Rory was sure it wasn't by choice.

"Why are you doing this to me, to our family?"

Rory slowed to a stop outside the dining room's entrance, obscured from view behind the half-opened sliding doors as their voices echoed loud of enough for her to hear.

"You could have had any one of the debutantes in our social circle, yet y—"

"Yet, I'm not interested in anyone else except, Rory. The

woman that I love, Mom," James spoke up, his statement bringing a smile to Rory's lips.

"She is a Kindergarten teacher, for God's sake," Lenora half-shouted. "Richard...tell him."

There was a pause before the elder Davis spoke up, "What your mother said, son."

"Can you imagine what our friends and family would say about this?" Lenora asked. "And to have the wedding in Oak Harbor. Really? Why don't we just have a good ol' back of woods, country hoe down of a wedding then?" Her voice dripped with disdain.

Rory shook her head in disbelief at how disrespectful her to be mother-in-law was being behind her back. It shouldn't have been surprising, but to hear her say those things still felt like being socked in the gut.

"Mom," James shot in a warning tone. "I am marrying the woman of my dreams. That's what should matter...that's what our family should be focusing on, and quite frankly, it's none of their business," he fumed with finality.

Instead of conceding, the woman tried another tactic of reasoning. "James, I know it might not seem to be of consequence now, but this union has the potential to wreck our family's reputation."

James released a frustrated breath as he asked, "How do you propose it will do that, mother?"

"Well, think of the information that just came to light. She is the product of a one-night stand to state the obvious, and to make matters worse, her mother fooled around with a married man."

Rory clutched her chest as her heart plummeted to the bottom of her chest. She couldn't hear anything else that Lenora was saying as the hurtful words kept ringing in her ears. It felt like the first time she'd met James' parents all over again, only the pain and shame from Lenora's words hit ten times greater. As much as she knew that her mother-in-law did not care for her, she'd thought that they were making progress enough to at least be tolerant of each other. The woman's attack on her mother and origin proved that she was unwilling to welcome Rory into her family and probably never would. Unshed tears burned her eyes as her vision became blurry. She pressed her fingers against her closed eyes, willing the tears away.

Rory took a deep breath and allowed her hands to fall by her sides. She walked through the open door, her expression as neutral as she could muster. She raised a questioning brow at James, who was on his feet, his expression dour.

"This dinner is over. We're leaving," he spoke, shocking her and the other two occupants at the table. James walked toward her, took her hand and all but hauled her toward the front door. A few minutes after the valet handed James the key to his Land Rover, they were driving through the gates of his parents' home.

"Are you okay?" Rory asked worriedly after more than ten minutes of tense silence.

"Yeah, I just...I have a lot on my mind," James responded, his voice tight.

"And you're angry," Rory concluded.

James released a long sigh. He looked at her briefly before turning his attention back to the road. "I'm sorry we had to leave like that," he told her a few seconds later. "My parents and I had a disagreement, and I didn't think it was wise to continue with our evening."

"Was it about me?" she slowly asked, even though she already knew the answer.

James's hand tightened on the steering, and a muscle ticked in his jaw. That was confirmation enough for her. Reaching across the console, she held his free hand. "I'm sorry."

"It's not your fault," he responded gruffly. He released a

heavy breath, and she felt him tense. James moved his hand from under hers and rested on the steering, looking straight ahead.

Rory turned to look at the dark, blurry figures the car zipped past. Her heart felt heavy with disappointment and fear.

It felt like James was pulling away from her.

Chapter One

Present Day

"Lenora, I don't want to change my color scheme and to be honest, adding orange will only throw off the theme entirely. Jennifer said she'd already spoke to you about this." Rory pinched the bridge of her nose and rested the back of her head against the wall. Her eyes were tightly shut, her brows drawn together in exasperation. She could feel a headache coming on as she tried to reason with the obstinate woman at the other end of the call. The only thing left for her to do was huff in annoyance at how difficult the woman was being.

"I thought you were okay with me offering input in this wedding. After all, it's my one and only son's first nuptials."

Rory's eyes flew open, only so she could roll them in irritation.

Lenora continued, "As much as I wanted the wedding to

take place here, it's not, and I have come to terms with it. I would therefore expect a little bit more gratitude. Yet, it feels like you're bent on excluding me and my ideas even though I have taken into consideration your situation and Richard and I have chosen to take care of everything, foregoing the tradition where the bride's parents pay for the wedding."

Rory felt like screaming at the woman in that instant. Instead, she turned and bumped her forehead against the wall with enough strength to feel the impact but not enough to hurt. She wished she didn't have to wait another couple of months before she could get her hands on the inheritance left to her. Then she wouldn't have to take Lenora's snide comments and her always throwing the fact that she and her husband were the ones paying for the wedding.

"All right, Lenora, if you think orange should be a part of the wedding, we'll find a way to incorporate it," she conceded. She was tired of the back and forth, and it was already decided that she would not win against the woman.

"Perfect," her mother-in-law replied, satisfied.

"I'm sorry. I have to go now. I have to mark some worksheets and prepare for my lesson tomorrow," she said, her tone dismissive.

"No worries, we'll speak more about the other changes I think you should make in the week," Lenora replied cheerily.

Rory grimaced. "Okay, bye Lenora."

"Bye, dear."

Rory released a long, exaggerated sigh the minute she disconnected the call. It felt like she'd just gotten out of the ring with a heavyweight boxing champion. She sauntered across the hardwood, cherry-stained floor of the living room to station herself at the floor-to-ceiling glass wall in the luxury apartment. She folded her arms across her chest and stared at the panoramic view of the city's urban landscape. From her vantage point, she could see the summits of Twin Peaks, the dome of City Hall and the skyscrapers of the financial district that permeated the skyline. The orange-pink hue dancing across the horizon made it even more spectacular as the sun set just beyond the bay, casting the buildings into more colorful but shadowy shades.

She wondered what time James would be getting in. He'd already been on an unpredictable schedule over the past month, which saw him getting in even later as time progressed. After heaving another long sigh, she crossed over to the kitchen island, where her work for the evening was already out. Three hours later, she was finished, but James still wasn't home. Packing up her things, she headed for the ensuite bathroom in their bedroom and ran herself a bath.

Rory heaved a sigh of relief as she submerged herself in the welcoming warmth of the water, the foamy bubbles settling over her. She rested her head against the tub's edge as she became more relaxed. She could already feel the tingling from the essential oils she'd added, and the tight muscles in her shoulders and arms had begun to unwind. She spent the next twenty minutes doing nothing but focusing on her breathing as the warm water performed its magic.

Her mind switched to James. She wished her fiancé was here to share this moment with her. She missed him. It was as if something had shifted in him after their last dinner with his parents. He was different somehow, and it was affecting their intimacy. For the umpteenth time, the niggling doubt in the back of her mind surfaced. Shaking her head to dispel the thought, she released a heavy breath as she pulled herself up out of the water. After securing the towel around her, she pulled the plug to release the water and made her way into the bedroom. After donning her pajamas, she exited the room.

"You're home," she spoke, surprised to find James posted by the glass-paneled wall.

James inclined his head in her direction. "Hey," he greeted, a barely there smile turning up the corners of his lips.

"Hey," Rory returned, her voice just above a whisper. "Did you just get in?" she asked, heading for the kitchen just at the other corner of the open floor plan of the space. "I was in the bath for about half-hour," she tacked on, opening the refrigerator, and removing the dish in saran wrap.

"I just got in a few minutes ago," he revealed, still stationed by the wall.

"I made chicken lasagna," she lifted off the wrap to place the dish in the microwave.

"I'm not hungry. I ate at the office," James replied.

"Oh...okay." Rory couldn't hide the disappointment in her voice.

"I'll just take it for lunch tomorrow," James added.

"That's okay. I know you've been busy. I should have expected that you would have eaten already." She mustered a smile. It felt more like a grimace. She wondered what it looked like to him.

She took a seat by the island. Her gaze remained fixed on her clasped hands until she heard the movement of the chair on the opposite side of her. She looked up as James took a seat. His expression looked troubled.

"How was your day?" she asked.

"Busy," he answered, his blue gaze cutting away from her.

"Okay," she answered, unsure of how to proceed after his abrupt response. "Well, I had a great day at work today," she told him.

"That's good," James responded half-heartedly as he reached into his pocket to retrieve the vibrating phone.

"Yeah. The children were super-excited to draw and paint pictures of their families. It surprised me how good some of them were. There was this one particular kid, though..." She chuckled at the memory. "He was—"

Her face fell, and the words died in her throat as she watched her fiancé fiddle with his phone.

"Apparently, whatever you're reading is far more important than you listening to me," she expressed in a deadpan voice.

James' blue eyes shot up to stare back at her guiltily. "Rory—"

Just then, her phone rang, the ringtone signaling that it was her mother calling. "I need to take that. Excuse me." She stepped out from behind her chair and crossed over to the living room. Reaching down, she retrieved her phone before pressing the answer button, then placed the phone against her ear.

"Hi, Mom," she greeted.

"Hi, sweetie. I know it's late, but you were on my mind, so I just wanted to check in and see how you're doing," her mother said. Even without her saying it outright, Rory could sense her concern.

"I'm fine, Mom. Everything's..." she cast her eyes to James, who was already staring back at her. "Everything's great," she lied, turning her back to look out at the high-rise buildings flooded with light.

"That's good to know," Andrea returned. "And how is my wonderful son-in-law? Is he there?"

Rory struggled to maintain an airy tone. "He's great. He's here but busy."

"Okay, well, tell him hi for me and not to work himself to death."

"I will, Mom," she promised, casting a look over her shoulder to see her fiancé's head resting on the island. "How are Aunt Cora and Aunt Jo? How is Grandma?" she asked, changing the subject.

"Cora and Jo are fine," Andrea replied. Her mother's hesitance in responding to her second question told her that Grandma Becky wasn't doing well.

"Mom's okay for the most part," Andrea finally answered after a long pause. "She's been far less active after the fall and her hairline fracture, but we're monitoring her."

Rory sighed sadly. "I wish there was a cure for this, Mom," she expressed.

"I know, sweetie. Me too," her mother agreed. "Enough about that. I know the wedding is a month and a half away, but I wish I was there with you every step of the way in planning it all."

Rory smiled, touched by the earnestness in her mother's voice.

"I remember promising you when you were eight that I would help you every step of the way to plan your wedding to Prince Charming."

Rory chuckled as the memory of that day came back so fresh in her mind. "I remember," she confirmed.

"Oh, sweetie...I'll make some time to come out to San Fran to help you with as much of the plans as I can, I promise."

"Mom, that's okay. You don't have to do that. You're needed in Oak Harbor, and I understand, I promise." Rory pressed the phone tightly against her ear as a wave of melancholy hit her. "Besides, James' mother is very much involved in the planning," she informed her.

"Oh, okay, sweetie." Her mother's disappointment gnawed at her.

"But don't worry, we'll still have plenty to plan together when I get to Oak Harbor," she assured the woman.

Hearing the pull and thud of a door, she looked over at the island to see it empty. James was no longer there. "Listen, Mom. I don't mean to end the call quickly, but I still have some finishing touches to make to my lesson."

"Okay, sweetie, I'll let you get back to it," Andrea conceded.

"Bye, mom."

"By sweetie."

Rory sighed deeply before heading toward the master bedroom. The bathroom door was partially opened, and she could hear the shower going. She sat up in the bed with her legs crossed as she waited for James. Three minutes later, the shower turned off and five minutes after that, James emerged from the bathroom in his pajama and a towel hanging loosely around his neck as he used one end to dry the excess water from his dirty blond hair. He stopped midway when he noticed her and the gravity on her face.

"What's wrong?" he asked.

"You're seriously asking me that?" Her eyes narrowed as she stared back at him.

James didn't respond.

Rory threw her hands in the air as annoyance got the better of her.

"How about the fact that you've been completely distant and distracted for nearly a month now. You don't look at me the way you used to...you don't look at me at all if I'm being honest. I miss our early morning cuddles and talks because, by the time I'm up, you're gone and don't get me started on how late you've been coming home." Rory huffed, the weight of her words affecting her mood.

She turned hurt green eyes on him as she said in a pained voice. "You don't even kiss me like you used to...It's like... we're two strangers occupying the same space at this point." Her eyes slid shut as she released a soft sigh. She opened them to see James staring back at her, guilt written all over his face.

"What happened to us, James?" she breathed out.

His gaze fell to his feet. His Adam's apple bobbed as he swallowed. "I need to show you something." He walked over to his briefcase and pulled out a file jacket.

"Now?" Rory asked, confused as to how this related to their

conversation. She moved to the edge of the bed and swung her legs over the edge, then stood up.

James turned back to her; his expression guarded. "I've been trying to find ways to give this to you for over two weeks now." He opened the file and handed it to her.

Rory reached for it with shaky hands. She felt drops of sweat form on her brow at how nervous she was. Carefully she began to read the words on the first page of the document. Her eyes widened into saucers before narrowing and tightening at the corners.

"What the heck is this?" she asked, gripping the paper as she looked back at James.

He released a shaky breath before replying. "It's a...um...a prenup. Mom and dad thought it was a good idea to have one just in case things don...things don't work out between us. They had our lawyers draw up the contract for us to sign," he rambled, then palmed the back of his neck.

"The fact that you've had this for so long and that you're actually giving it to me only means that you're in agreement with them."

He didn't reply, but only stared back at her, his face riddled with guilt.

Rory felt her heart lodge in her ribs as her chest tightened with pain and her insides screamed out from the affliction and betrayal she felt.

"Oh my God," she exclaimed, just as her hand flew to her mouth to stifle the guttural sound that threatened to leave her lips.

She shook her head, then stood up and ran into the living room leaving James alone in the bedroom before she'd return for round two of the argument.

How could he have done this to her?

Chapter Two

"Com'on, Drea. You've been thinking about your bet for a whole two minutes now. Either call or fold."

Andrea looked between the two cards in her hand, then at the four currently facing up on the table before looking around the table at the expectant and impatient faces staring back at her.

"Let her be Kerry. That is the mark of a true poker player—taking the time to consider all the odds before making your move," Luke directed at his daughter, who sat at the table with a dour expression on her face as she listened to him.

Andrea chuckled at their interaction and turned her attention to her hand. "All right, I'm calling," she finally decided. Picking up two of the chips from her heap, she placed them with the others already stacked in the middle of the table.

"Finally," Kerry sighed in relief. There were other collective sighs of relief as the play passed to Jo on her left. Andrea playfully rolled her eyes while a smirk raised the corners of her lips.

"Check," Jo said almost immediately, holding the cards close to her chest.

Soon enough, it was Andrea's turn again, and this time she didn't hesitate to raise the stake after the last card was placed beside the other four.

"I don't like the sound of that. I'm folding," Jo returned, laying her hand of cards on the table and leaning back in her chair.

"I'm folding too," Tessa, who sat to her immediate left, decided a few seconds later.

"Me too," came the decisions of her two Aunts, her mother and Julia.

"There is no way you have such a great hand with what's on the table," Kerry challenged.

Andrea simply inclined her head to the right with a teasing smirk on her lips as her cousin stared pointedly at her, trying to determine if she was bluffing. Reaching for her cup of coffee, she sipped it, unbothered.

"You're the one holding up the game now, Kare Bear," she threw mockingly at her cousin, her lips once more turned up in what was becoming her signature smirk.

"Remind me why we play poker again?"

It was Julia who had spoken this time, her hand rubbing her rounded belly as she brought the croissant to her lips and took a bite.

"Because it is a family tradition to play poker every Sunday, sweetie. Besides, it's a healthy dose of clean fun," Cora expressed to her daughter.

"If you say so. But Aunt Andrea and Kerry look like they're on the verge of coming to blows," she returned, bringing the table's attention back to the two cousins staring unblinkingly at each other from across the table like it's a showdown.

"You know, we won't call you a coward if you choose to fold Kerry," Andrea threw at her cousin.

"You know what?" Kerry squinted in determination. "There's no way your hand is that great, and I know my hand isn't shabby either, so I'm calling your bluff."

Kerry took up the extra chips and threw them into the pile.

Andrea smiled, self-satisfied and turned her attention to Uncle Luke, the only other player still in the game. "What are you going to do, Uncle Luke?"

Luke looked at his hand, then back at the cards on the table. Frown lines creased the corners of his mouth. "Hmm." He looked at his hand once more. "I'm calling it too," he finally decided and added his chips to the pile as well.

Andrea smiled triumphantly as she placed her two cards on the table facing up. "Beat that."

Kerry gaped in disbelief.

Luke stroked his chin contemplatively.

"Come on, Kerry. Let's see what you have."

Kerry's mouth snapped shut as she recovered from her sudden stupor and drew in a thin line as she revealed her own hand. "I guess you win," she said lowly.

"Ooh, what's that? I can't hear you," Andrea snickered, cupping her hand behind her ear.

"You win, Drea," Kerry deadpanned.

"Hold on now, sweetheart. Your father hasn't revealed his hand as yet, so we can't make that declaration just yet," Maria but in, smiling over at her husband, who Andrea now realized with dread had a glint in the corner of his blue eyes.

"You're right, honey, we can't," he agreed before revealing his own hand.

This time it wasn't just Kerry's mouth that flopped open, but Andrea's as well, along with a few surprised gasps that rang out around the table.

"I don't know how you do it, Uncle Luke, but you are hands down the best player I've ever known," Andrea complimented.

"Thank you, dear. You're not bad yourself," Luke returned.

"If we keep this up, pretty soon you'll be gunning for the top spot."

"Hey, what about me?" Kerry interjected, her lower lip jutting out to a pout.

"You're also exceptional, sweetie," Luke placated, then gave her a wink.

"There," Kerry threw back at her cousin, poking her tongue out.

Andrea stuck her tongue back out. The two ended up making funny faces at each other before bursting into laughter. Those at the table joined in.

"Ready for another round?" Cora asked.

"You bet."

"Yes," came the collective agreement of everyone else.

Cora collected the free cards to complete the pack. After a few shuffles, she began dealing the players' hands. Andrea bit into her croissant as she waited.

"So, Thanksgiving is only three weeks away. Me, Jo, and Drea were discussing it with Mom, and we think that maybe we should have it here at the main house with all of the family," Cora suggested.

"I think that that's a marvelous idea," Maria agreed.

"Me too," Aunt Stacey chimed in. "We haven't had a Thanksgiving dinner with everyone together as a family in more than two decades."

"I am definitely all for it, reviving family traditions and all," Tessa added.

The others nodded or murmured their agreements for the plan.

"So, it's settled then. Thanksgiving will be here," Cora concluded.

"Speaking of events coming up, Drea, for Rory's wedding, can I take a plus one?"

Andrea looked over at her cousin, staring back at her expectantly. "I'll have to discuss it with her, but I don't see it being a problem," she replied. A mischievous glint appeared in her eyes. "Is this an indication that you and Ethan are taking your relationship to the other level?"

"I wouldn't call it, "taking the next step," we've already done that," Kerry explained. Her green eyes shone with contentment. Seeing her father's narrowed, questioning stare, she rushed on, "What I mean to say is that we've made it official. We're exclusively dating, getting to know each other, going on dates, nothing more."

Luke's shoulders relaxed as he slumped back into his chair and the crow's feet at the corners of his eyes smoothed out.

"He's not coming with me; he's going to a conference on the 23rd of December."

"The same day as Rory's wedding," Andrea pointed out.

"Yeah," Kerry confirmed. "I wanted to take Ella because I want her to get to know us better."

"That's a good idea. In that case, you can definitely bring a plus one," Andrea assured her.

Kerry smiled gratefully.

"Man, the days seem to be melding into each other. Christmas will be here sooner than we think, and then the new year..."

Andrea nodded her head to agree with Cora.

"Time is a precious gift that we have to appreciate no matter how short it may be. I'm just happy that we'll be getting to spend it a-ll together as a f-f-f-amily," Becky added softly.

Andrea stared at her mother, her expression bitter-sweet. As happy as she was that she had reconnected with Becky before it was too late, it pained her heart to know that any day now, her illness would get worse and sooner than later, the inevitable would happen. Fear surfaced like a dark cloud that threatened to swallow all the joy of the moment they'd been having until now. She tried hard to swallow over the lump in her throat.

Cora looked over at her, her expression telling. "I'm happy we get to spend it together as a family, too, Mom. I know that these family get-togethers will be some of the best we've ever had." She reached across the table to rest her hand on top of Becky's reassuringly.

Andrea felt Jo's warm palm rest on the hand, gripping her thigh under the table. She turned to see her sister staring back at her, a barely there smile of understanding on her lips. She managed to return it, drawing strength and comfort from the simple gesture.

Suddenly there was an outburst of laughter. Andrea's eyes snapped to the other end of the table to stare at her mother. Becky seemed oblivious to the attention she was receiving even as she cackled uncontrollably, but just as unexpectedly, her chortles became whimpers until she was full-out crying.

"Mom," Cora spoke in alarm, rising from her seat to go to her. "Hey, what's wrong?" she cajoled as she knelt by Becky's side.

Andrea's legs felt like jelly, and her heart hammered in her chest. Slowly she made her way over to her mother until she too was kneeling before her. Becky was now whimpering, her eyes wide with fear.

"Mom, we're here for you. Tell us what's wrong...please." Andrea's voice broke as she pleaded.

Even though Becky's mouth opened as if to speak, no words came out.

"Girls, maybe a few hours of rest would be best for Becky," Uncle Luke suggested from above them. "I'll take her up to her room," he offered. The women stepped away from Becky and allowed Luke to bundle her in his arms and take her up the stairs. The sisters followed him up after bidding goodbye to their cousins and aunts. After Uncle Luke left, they gathered around their mother, who had fallen asleep.

"I think we should take her to the doctor," Cora suggested after a length of silence.

"I think so, too," Jo agreed.

Andrea simply nodded, still overcome by emotions to utter any words.

* * *

"I'm gonna check on mom."

Andrea nodded before watching Jo exit the kitchen to head upstairs. She released a labored breath and turned back to making a pureed fruit shake for her mother. As soon as Cora returned from the inn, they would be heading to the doctor's office. The day prior had been hard to watch Becky's behavior during their poker game and they were getting very concerned.

Fifteen minutes later, Jo and her mother hadn't come down the stairs. Putting the shake in the refrigerator, she made her way upstairs.

"Jo, what's taking so…"

Jo knelt before her mother, who was bent over the edge of the bed.

"Her hand," Jo pointed out with alarm. Andrea's eyes immediately locked on her mother's hand, where her fingers curled inwards toward her palm. "It's stuck. I can't get them straight and…"

"Jo, it's fine," Andrea reassured, helping her to her feet. "Everything will be fine."

"Mom, does it hurt?" she asked her mother whose eyes had been downcast.

Andrea's heart felt like it would shatter at the hurt and fear embedded in her mother's light brown eyes as they raised to meet hers. "I'm sorry," she murmured, her voice cracking on the last syllable.

Andrea rushed over to hug her close. "It's fine, Mom. None of this is your fault. We'll be here for you through it all. I promise."

Twenty minutes later, Cora was back, and they piled into her Land Rover and took off. A half-hour later, they were seated in Doctor Muller's office while he examined their mother.

"All right, there is no easy way to say this, but...your mother's symptoms have progressed to stage 2 of the disease," the doctor briefed them. "What that means is that she will be having far more of these episodes and a lot worse. It comes with a lot of pain, swelling and stiff muscles, and in some instances, eating will be difficult because the mouth will have less and less saliva. ALS is extremely aggressive once it gets to this stage, so it won't be long before it progresses to stage three. You would be lucky if you get more than two months tops before it gets there."

"What can we do? There must be something..." Cora asked, the desperation causing her voice to rise.

Doctor Muller sighed. "I'm afraid there is nothing more medically that can be done," he revealed. Looking seriously around the room at them, he said, "You need to spend as much time as you can with Becky, making happy memories and getting her as comfortable as possible. Once it gets to stage three, she will only be a shell of herself."

On the ride home, the sisters remained silent as they mulled over all that the doctor had revealed. Andrea looked over at her mother, whose eyes were closed as she rested her head against the seat. A tear slipped down her cheek as helplessness tore her apart inside.

"I can't believe this is happening," Andrea breathed out feeling a tear slip down her cheek.

A Spectacular Event

Cora released a tired, defeated sigh while Jo remained silent. When they arrived home, they helped Becky upstairs to rest. As soon as she'd fallen asleep, they chose to have a cup of tea out on the side porch.

"As much as I wish it wasn't, we have to make plans now to keep Mom comfortable and safe," Cora spoke, looking at each sister.

"I think we should install a lift for the stairs," Jo suggested.

"Or move her bedroom to the first floor," Andrea countered.

Cora nodded contemplatively. "We'll need to install some cameras too, and someone will have to be with her twenty-four-seven."

The sisters nodded in agreement.

"Do you think...she's aware of what's coming?" Jo asked, worried.

Cora pursed her lips as tears welled up in her eyes. She looked out across the bay as her tears began falling. Andrea turned to look out at the bay as her own tears slipped through their barriers to cascade down her cheeks. Soon the three sisters sat, staring straight ahead as silent tears flowed.

Chapter Three

"I can't believe you're asking me to sign this. After all, we've been through..." Rory paced the floor as she struggled to reign in her anger. James watched her, his lips glued together.

Suddenly she stopped pacing to stare at him with hurt in the depths of her green eyes. "You don't trust me."

"That's not true, Rory. I trust you with my entire life," James rushed out. He walked toward her but stopped a few centimeters away. James sighed, running his hand over his already disheveled hair in frustration and angst. "The prenup wasn't my idea. I never thought about having a prenup. All I've ever wanted is to marry you." He stared at her, his eyes shining with earnest feelings.

"It wasn't your idea, but it sure didn't stop you from giving it to me," she said, giving him a deadpan expression.

James opened and closed his mouth, unable to come up with an appropriate response.

"You're allowing your parents to control our lives, your mother specifically, and you can't even see it." She shook her head in disappointment and turned her back to him. "They're controlling your life, James," she stated.

"That's not true, Rory. I love you, and I'm marrying you. No matter what, I'll always choose to marry you," James spoke softly.

Rory whirled to look at him directly. "The fact that, that is the only thing you're able to say you're in control of, is both sad and frustrating to me."

James' blue eyes widened.

"Lenora has been wrecking our wedding plans with her own ideas, and you've done nothing to stop it. Did you know that she called insisting that I had to have orange at my wedding even though it didn't match the theme? She wants me to have an eight-tier cake even though I told her four tiers was how high I was willing to go, and don't get me started on the flowers." Rory huffed, folding her arms over her chest as the memory of her mother-in-law's bullish antics riled her. "The only thing left for her to do is take over the designing of the invitations and choosing who makes it onto the guestlist."

James' eyes shuttered before they opened to stare back at her, determination in their blue depths. "If you don't like the changes she's making, all you have to say is, no."

Rory favored him with an angry glint her eye. "It's like you've not been listening to a single word I have been saying. Your mother doesn't like me. Do you want her to hate me more? Because that's what'll happen if I choose not to agree with her ideas."

"Rory," James started, the weariness in his voice telling her he was not in agreement with her statement. "Mom doesn't hate you. She's just...careful. She has..." James looked away from her.

"She has what?" Rory pressed.

"She has doubts that we will last," he finished after a few seconds of silence.

Rory felt as if she'd been sucker punched in the gut. "Judging by the way you are reluctant to see what she has been doing to me and call her out on it, hurts so much. But the catalyst to all of this is the fact that you brought home a prenup and now stand before me defending her— it's clear to me that you agree with what she's doing."

"Rory, that's not wh—"

"You know what, James? I'm tired, and it's evident that this is going nowhere. When it comes to a decision between your mother and me, I will never win because as much as you have been saying how much I matter to you, I matter less than her, and I'm the woman you're supposed to be getting ready to spend the rest of your life with," she argued, her voice cracking from the overwhelming hurt of the realization in her words caused. She felt a sole tear roll down her cheek.

James opened his mouth to speak, but she held up her hand, stopping him. "I just need to be alone right now," she spoke in finality.

"I'll sleep in the guest bedroom then," James replied after some time of staring at Rory, who refused to look back at him.

The moment the door closed after his exit, Rory's breath caught in her throat, then she felt the rush of tears spill over like the hoover dam. What was supposed to be shaping up to be the happiest moment of her life was instead heading toward what could only be labeled a disaster. Turning to the bed, she slowly slid into it and hugged a pillow to her chest as she screamed her frustration into the plush sound absorber.

The pinging of her phone caused her to raise her head to look for it. Noticing the device on the bedside table, she reached over and grabbed it. It was a text from her father's lawyer letting her know that the funds would be released to her hopefully sooner than the expected date. Hopefully, she would get it by Christmas.

Relief washed over her but it was quickly replaced by

sadness once more. She hadn't shared that bit of news with James yet. Now she wasn't sure she wanted to tell him about the money; she wasn't even sure there would be a wedding come December 23rd. Tears welled up in her eyes before flowing once more. She pulled the pillow to her face, muffling her cries.

The next morning James was gone before she was up. A wave of disappointment washed over her that he hadn't stayed and tried to work out their problems. Tamping down the emotion, she willed herself to have a great day at work. She would, after all, be seeing her lovely students who always managed to cheer her up by being their loving, authentic selves.

After getting ready, she filled her travel mug with coffee and grabbed an apple to go.

"You're doing great, Peter. Keep up the good work."

The little boy beamed up at her, revealing the empty space where his two front teeth once were.

"What about mine, Miss Hamilton?"

Rory turned to the little girl with pigtails whose expectant brown eyes stared back at her as she held up her painting for review.

"That is well done, Chelsea. Good job," she complimented the little girl, earning a toothy smile from her also. It caused her own lips to turn up in a warm smile.

So far, the day had been going great. Her students were doing exceptionally well, and it made her heart swell with pride.

"All right, children, as soon as you're done, please show Miss McCallister or me what you've done."

For the next half hour, her students completed their artwork and eagerly showed it, reveling in the praises they received.

"All right, guys, it's recess time."

"Yay!"

Rory smiled at their eagerness to head outside. "Pack away your things, and we can head outside."

"Are you okay, Rory?"

She looked at her friend and colleague, staring back at her with concern.

"I'm fine, Amber. Just a little tired. I didn't get much sleep last night." Rory tacked on a smile to reassure her.

"I can imagine with your wedding less than two months away," Amber reasoned.

The smile on Rory's face slipped a little.

"But don't worry, it'll be worth it because you're marrying the man of your dreams, and I'm sure it's bound to be a fairytale even," Amber continued, oblivious of the turmoil brewing on her inside. "I'm just happy that I'll get to witness it. I am still getting an invitation, right?"

"Of course," Rory informed her.

"Good." Amber's smile grew, her brown eyes bright and filled with relief.

Rory moved toward the door to direct her students outside, but Amber stopped her with a hand on her arm. She looked over at her questioningly.

"I'll take them outside. You can take a quick nap. I've got you," she offered.

Rory's lips curled into a grateful smile. "Thanks. I owe you one."

Amber returned her smile. "Don't mention it."

As soon as Amber and the students had all filed out of the classroom, the exhaustion from her fight with James and the sleepless night she'd had hit her like a moving truck. Rory heaved a heavy sigh as she sank into the chair at her desk. Just as she was about to rest her head on the desk, her phone rang. Removing it from her bag, she looked at the caller id before answering.

"Hi, Mom."

"Hi, sweetie. I'm glad I got you," Andrea greeted.

"Why, is something wrong?" Rory perked up.

"No, no...not really. I just called to see if you're okay. Last night...I know you said you were fine, but...you sounded a bit off, and I was worried."

"I'm fine, Mom. I'm just...tired. It's been busy since I got back from Oak Harbor with lesson prepping and planning for the wedding. I guess I've just been a bit overwhelmed. Plus, James has been quite busy too..." she trailed off. Coils of guilt knotted her stomach. She'd always been able to tell her mother anything, but now she just couldn't get the words past her throat to tell her that it was more than just fatigue plaguing her. It had been that way since she found out Andrea had lied to her about her father.

"Why don't you take some time off work and come visit Oak Harbor? I'm sure Amber won't mind taking over the class for a bit, and, I can help you with the rest of your wedding list... think about it."

Rory thought about her mother's suggestion and couldn't see why not. Maybe some time away from James and his toxic parents would do her some good.

"That's actually a good idea, Mom," she agreed. "I just need Mrs. Connelly to sign off on it."

"Great, I can't wait to see you," Andrea breathed out in relief.

"Mom...are you sure everything is fine?"

There was a short pause before her mother spoke.

"It's Mom...we had to take her to the doctor. She had an episode and..."

There was a heavy sigh. Rory worried her bottom lip as she waited for her mother to continue.

"She's at stage two of the disease Rory, and pretty soon it will progress to stage three and then..."

Rory's heart constricted with sadness. She knew what her

mother feared to say, and it pained her to know that soon, her grandmother would be gone.

"I'm so sorry, Mom."

"Me too, sweetie," Andrea replied, her voice tight with regret. "All we can do now is make sure she's comfortable and surrounded by family."

"I will definitely be there then."

As soon as she was off the phone, Rory switched on her laptop and emailed her superior to request time off.

Two days later, Rory zipped her carry-on with a sigh of relief that everything she'd planned to take with her had fit in the small luggage. She wheeled the suitcase out of her bedroom and posted it by the front door. Removing the letter from her laptop bag, she walked over to the kitchen island. She stared at the folded paper for a long time before finally placing it on the counter.

The sound of the alarm system disarming caused her to turn toward the door just as James walked through. He stopped in his tracks, his hand on the doorknob as he stared at Rory, who was already staring at him, surprised. She hadn't expected him home. *Why was he home so early?* Suddenly his gaze cut to the suitcase just inches from his feet before looking questioningly back at her.

"Are you going somewhere?"

Rory recovered from her stupor in time to respond. "I took some time off from work. I'm going to Oak Harbor."

"Were you planning on leaving without telling me?" His voice was deadly calm, but his eyes flared with restrained anger.

Her own anger came to the surface. "I didn't think there was anything to tell. We've both been doing our own thing. I've literally only said ten words to you in the past two days. I've counted."

"So what? I would have just come home to an empty house and wondered if you were okay. How can y—"

"Look, James, I really don't have the time for this," she breathed tiredly. "I was planning on leaving a letter for you, but you're here now. I need some time away from...this," she gestured between them. "I'm going to Oak Harbor because it's the only place where I won't feel like I'm alone. Plus, I need to spend time with my grandmother, who doesn't have much time left."

James stared at her for a beat. His Adam's apple bobbed as he swallowed, and his eyes became hooded. "Okay." With that, he moved away from the door, granting her exit.

Rory walked over to her luggage, hesitating over the handle before she wrapped her palm around it and walked out of the apartment.

In her car, she aggressively hit the steering over and over again before resting her head against it as hot tears streamed down her cheeks and her heart threatened to burst in two.

Chapter Four

Rory yawned for the fourth time since leaving San Francisco eight hours ago. She was starting to regret her impulsive decision to drive all the way to Whidbey Island rather than take the plane. At the rate she was going and the exhaustion she felt, she was sure she would be asleep within the next hour. It was time to find a motel. Pulling up her map, she browsed the ones in close proximity to Portland's I-5 N. She chose Sunnyside Inn, which was only a mile away from the highway.

A half-hour later, she was settled under the warm covers of a four-poster bed. The next morning at the crack of dawn, she was back on the road, and in five hours, she was driving over the Deception Pass Bridge. Each time she'd driven over it or viewed it from the State Park, she'd been in awe. The majestic structure curved beautifully over the blue-green water below and provided a panoramic view of the landmasses populated with evergreens and deciduous trees that connected to the mainland and surrounded by the pacific.

She needed to paint it and the Cascade Mountains, which

would be trading its evergreen palette soon enough for one marked by snow-capped peaks juxtaposed against a clear, blue sky. There was so much that she appreciated about this small town and wished she could pack up and take it back with her to San Fran.

Two minutes later, she'd driven past the elliptical welcome sign that displayed the words 'Welcome to Whidbey Island' in bold, black letters and ten minutes after that, she was driving through the famous avenue of Oaks. Oak trees lined either side of the street like guard rails.

When she finally pulled past the sign that read 'Willberry Inn, Restaurant and Property,' anticipation bubbled on the inside, and she slowed the car to give herself enough time to get her emotions in check. She took the time to admire her surroundings. Colorful leaves floated to the ground as she passed the Oak and Birch trees preparing for the winter. A pile of leaves stood tall under one. She remembered how back in New York, she'd wished she had things like these— mountains of leaves to play in. She passed well-maintained boxwood and fire, and ice daylilies led the way to the inn, a three-story colonial home renovated to incorporate a few modern architectural changes. Soon she was passing the restaurant with its rustic exterior and pulling up to the main house.

Drawing in a deep breath, she exhaled and exited her car. The air here, she noted, was a lot cooler than back in San Fran, and she found herself pulling her sweater tighter around her.

"Hi, sweetie," her mother greeted when she stepped out.

"Hi, Mom," Rory smiled, walking into her mother's embrace. The warmth and affection of the hug tugged at her heart, and she wanted to cry. It felt like coming home.

"Let's get you inside. You must be tired after all the driving," Andrea suggested after they separated.

"I'm not that tired. I stopped at that motel. Remember?"

"Okay. Well, you can just freshen up, and we can talk after that," she conceded.

"Where's grandma?" she asked the minute they stepped into the foyer.

Andrea hesitated. Rory could see the pain that flashed in her eyes before they became hooded.

"Mom's taking a nap, but she'll be down in the afternoon. You can greet her then."

Rory nodded her agreement.

Rory followed her mother upstairs to her room and freshened up. Andrea was seated on the chaise by the bed when Rory exited the bathroom.

"Is everything okay?" she asked.

"Yes," Andrea replied immediately. "David's lawyer called." Rory blinked back her surprise as she waited for her mother to continue. "He said your sister and brother would like to meet you."

"Why didn't he call me? He has my number, and I spoke with him a few days ago." Rory couldn't keep the annoyance out of her tone.

Andrea drew in a breath and released it before replying to her daughter's query. "Maybe it was an oversight or something different altogether. I'll make sure to tell him that all further correspondence goes only to you."

"Mom...I'm sorry. That didn't come out right." Rory felt bad for snapping at her. The hurt that flashed in her mother's blue eyes filled her with guilt. "I didn't mean to be so harsh. I don't know what came over me," she added.

Andrea smiled reassuringly. "It's fine. In truth, I should have directed him to you."

Rory inclined her head in acknowledgment, but she still felt bad about her reaction earlier. Reaching up, she removed the barrette holding the two braids she'd put her hair in. Her scalp needed liberation.

"Let me help you with that."

Rory walked over to her mother and plopped down on the soft, plush carpet before her mother. Andrea reached for one of the braids and began unraveling it by running her finger through the interwoven strands.

"I don't know if I want to meet them," she revealed after her mother had gotten started on the second braid.

"It's entirely up to you, sweetie. You can take your time to think about it. You don't have to rush to do anything right now."

Rory smiled appreciatively.

"Let's talk about something else," Andrea offered. "How is your job?"

"It's great. The children are wonderful." A warm smile came to her lips as she thought about them.

"I'm happy that you love what you do, sweetie," Andrea spoke sincerely.

"I do," she agreed. A purr of satisfaction left her lips as her mother massaged her scalp. "That feels so good."

"So how did that son-in-law of mine take the news that you'd be leaving him on his own for a while?"

The question caught Rory off guard and her heart hammered against her chest. "Um, he's...he's fine with it. He understood that I needed some time away," she answered carefully.

"That's...thoughtful. Is he planning on visiting before the week of the wedding?"

"James is very busy, Mom. He's got a high-profile case that he's working on, so I doubt that," she expressed.

Sweat pooled in her palms, and she prayed her mother's questions about James would stop.

There was a long pause as Andrea continued to run her fingers through her hair. "I'm happy you have each other."

Rory couldn't respond.

"What are you going to do about Grandma Becky?"

Andrea's fingers stilled. She released a low, shaky breath.

"We're still thinking about the best option, but we're already sourcing the equipment for assisted living."

"Does grandma know that the disease is spreading rapidly?"

"We explained to her that it's progressing but not how quickly."

Rory sighed. "I can't imagine how frightening this must be for her." She shuddered.

"It is frightening," Andrea agreed solemnly. "I'm gonna head downstairs. You can come down when you're ready."

"Thanks, Mom. I'll be down shortly."

Ten minutes after her mother left, Rory made her way downstairs. She found Aunt Cora and Grandma Becky in the living room watching a prerecorded episode of 'The Price is Right.'

"Hi, Aunt Cora."

Cora's eyes lit up at her presence, and she slipped off the couch to greet Rory. "Hi, honey. It's so good to see you."

"You too," Rory smiled.

When the two separated, Rory looked over at the small, frail-looking woman still seated on the couch, her brown eyes staring back at her.

"Hi, Grandma," she breathed softly out.

"Hi, dear," she greeted back with a small smile.

Rory took tentative steps toward her. She carefully lowered herself into the space her aunt had vacated and gently wrapped her arms around her grandmother's shoulders. Becky's thin arms came up to wrap around her back.

"How are you feeling?" Rory asked when they separated, her eyes fixed on Becky's face.

Her grandmother gave her a strained smile. "I could have been better, but I'm not complaining. I'm just glad that I get to have you all around me," she expressed, her voice small and wispy as if it took much effort for her to speak.

Rory hugged her once more. "I'm happy to hear that, grandma," she breathed out.

"Rory, your mom said to tell you if you need her, she's on the back porch," Cora informed her.

"Okay. Thanks, Aunt Cora. I'll let you guys get back to your show." Rory squeezed her grandmother's arm warmly before getting up and heading for the back door. She found Andrea sitting on the wicker chair, staring out at the harbor.

She walked over and sat in the chair closest. "Hi," she greeted.

"Hi." Andrea smiled over at her daughter. "Want one?" She held up the can of Root beer to her.

"No thanks," Rory declined.

The two sat in silence, comfortably staring out at the horizon. Hearing the creak of the door, the two looked over to see Julia stepping through it. Oblivious of their presence, she raised her hands above her head, slightly leaning forward as she released a tired groan.

"Oh, hi," she greeted the moment she saw them.

"Hi, Jules," Rory greeted her cousin.

"Hi, Rory. It's great to see you again."

Rory returned her smile with one of her own. "How's the baby?" she asked, her gaze landing on Julia's prominently rounded stomach.

Julia's hand automatically touched her belly. A haunted look flashed in her hazel eyes before disappearing. "The baby's fine," she responded, a facsimile of a smile on her lips. "I'm gonna go for a walk."

"Okay, sweetie," Andrea answered.

Rory wondered what that was about. "Is she okay?" she turned to ask Andrea.

"She's..." Andrea hesitated, unsure of what to say. "She's

going through a lot, but she doesn't talk about it. All we can do is be there for her and give her time," she finally explained.

Rory nodded. She understood that so well. Her heart went out to her cousin. "I think I'm gonna go for a walk too." She hoisted herself to her feet.

Andrea gave her a skeptical look.

"I'm just going for a walk, nothing more," she promised.

Her mother looked away. "Okay."

With that, Rory descended the three steps and headed in the opposite direction of where Julia had gone. She didn't make it back to the house until dinner time.

The minute she stepped through the door, the aroma that infiltrated her nostrils caused her to salivate, and her stomach growled in anticipation. She hadn't realized she was that hungry until now.

"Oh, good. You're back," her mother greeted her when she entered the kitchen. "We're about to sit to eat. You can wash up and come to the dining room," she instructed. She removed the apron she wore and lifted the green bean casserole into her hands and headed for the dining room.

Rory did as instructed, then headed upstairs to freshen up before returning to the main floor and into the dining room. When she entered, everyone was already seated around the table. She hurriedly took her seat.

"Could you pass the salt, please?"

Rory reached for the saltshaker and handed it to Julia before concentrating on her own plate.

"Don't you think that's a little bit too much, Jules?"

"Are you going to monitor my diet like everything else now?"

Rory looked up, surprised at the argument ensuing between mother and daughter. All other chatter ceased as the focus remained on the two.

"That's not... that's not what I'm trying to do, honey," Cora sighed defeatedly. "I only said what I said because, from experience, a high intake of sodium can affect your pregnancy and you."

Julia's hand tightened around the porcelain bottle she held, her knuckles appearing white. "You know what?" She placed the saltshaker back on the table and stood. "I think I lost my appetite. Please excuse me." Julia turned, then walked out of the room.

Cora, who had stared at her daughter's retreating back, slack-jawed, shook herself out of her stupor and stood to her feet. "Please excuse me." She left the table and went after her daughter.

"So, Rory, I'm really excited about baking the cake for your wedding," Kerry, who was also at the dinner, spoke up, trying to recenter the conversation. "I can't wait to show you the samples and have you taste them," she continued, her green eyes sparkling in excitement.

"I can't wait," Rory returned, her lips slightly upturned. She shifted her eyes to her plate.

"Have you found a dress yet?" Josephine asked.

"Not yet," she responded, stabbing a piece of the chicken, and putting it in her mouth.

Andrea stared at her daughter until their eyes locked. Rory noticed how her mother was watching the slight furrowing of her brows and probably how short her answers were the more they spoke about the wedding. She knew her mother thought something was definitely not right.

After supper, Rory flopped face down on the bed, exhausted. She hadn't anticipated all the questions about James and the wedding that she would be fielding and how taxing it would have been. Her vibrating phone caught her attention. Reaching her hand over to the bedside table, she ran her hand along the surface until it came in contact with the object.

"Hello?" she answered, not bothering to look at the caller id.

"Hi."

Rory sat up alert.

"Hey," she replied, her voice coming out breathy.

"How is Oak Harbor?"

"It's great...it's been great." After a short pause, she continued. "I'm glad I left the city. I needed this time away from our situation and from your mother to clear my head and put things into perspective." Her grip tightened around her cell phone; her breath held hostage in her chest as she waited for him to say something.

"And are they any clearer now?" he asked, his voice even.

Rory released her breath. "They are. Yes."

"What about our wedding?"

Rory sucked in a deep breath and slowly released it not saying a word. She had no words, only thoughts.

How did I get to this point in my life?

Chapter Five

One, two, three, one, two, three. Andrea counted in rhythm with her steps as her feet thumped the sand, displacing the tiny granules as she pushed forward. When the muscles in her legs began to tighten, and her breathing became choppy, she decelerated, coming to a stop a few seconds later. Bending over with her hands splayed on her legs, she drew in rapid breaths to replenish the depleted oxygen in her burning lungs. When she felt more relaxed, she straightened to look out at the deep blue waves, the snow-capped Olympic mountains appearing to rise out of the depths of the ocean against the pre-dawn sky in phantasmic style. She was happy she'd chosen to head out for her morning run as the clock struck five.

She stood with her arms flattened over her chest and soaked up the serenity of the view. Her mind traveled to one year ago. She'd been preparing to host the biggest technology launch of her career. Everything had been lining up in her favor. But then, her father died. That had been devastating enough as she considered the many times she had wanted to reach out to him to rebuild their relationship but hadn't. Then, she found out her mom was sick and that her father had left the inn and restaurant to her and her sisters.

The very thing that she had been running away from for more than half of her life was part of the reason she ended up moving back to Oak Harbor. She didn't regret coming back, though. She was given the chance to reconnect with her mother, her sisters, and the rest of the family, and it was far more important, more fulfilling than the offers she'd turned down. The bonus had been that she'd met and was steadily falling in love with a wonderful man who adored her and looked after her like no one else ever had. If anyone had told her that her life would look like it did now, she would have told them they didn't know what they were talking about. Everything was far better than she could have anticipated. She only wished that she'd known about her mother's condition way before when she did.

Maybe if she had, there would have been more time to find a clinical trial that could have accommodated her. Maybe, just maybe, it could have helped to prolong her life. Instead, her mother was running out of time, like sand in an hour glass, and there was nothing she could do. The helpless feeling tore at her heart. The sudden wave of sadness that enveloped her elicited a guttural cry from her lips as her hands went lower to wrap around her waist, holding herself together as the pain in her chest increased. Andrea turned her face skyward, the tears still flowing from the corners of her eyes.

"Dad...I miss you so much right now. I'm so sorry for taking so long to come back. If I had, then none of this...none of this would have." Andrea reached up, wiping at her tears. "None of this would have happened," she finally managed to say. "But I promise to be there for mom all the way to the end. I'll care for her just like how I know you would if you were still here.

Please, Dad... if you're hearing me, please make her time tolerable. Don't let mom go through this horrible pain."

Andrea shook her head to clear the fog of melancholy and regroup. Turning around, she lightly jogged in the direction of home. When she made it back to the house, she headed upstairs to take a shower and get started on breakfast. The sisters had decided to take turns preparing the meals and doing housework. Today was her day.

Andrea headed downstairs, contemplating what to prepare. The house was still silent, indicating that the others were probably still asleep. She headed for the kitchen. Opening the pantry, she removed the pancake mix before heading to the refrigerator for eggs, sausages, and turkey cold cuts. She placed the items on the counter and reached for a bowl and a whisk.

As she prepared the batter, a sound caught her attention. She stopped to investigate.

"I don't care what she wants, James."

Andrea's eyes widened in surprise at the anger in her daughter's tone. It was evident that she was talking to James but not why she was almost shouting at him, enough so that her voice carried all the way into the kitchen. It was then she noticed the screened door that led out to the side porch was slightly ajar. She went to close it but drew up short at Rory's next words.

"I am not changing the wedding venue. This is one thing I will not budge on. I have already compromised so much."

There was a long pause. Andrea inched closer to the door. She hadn't meant to eavesdrop, but she wouldn't have been able to help it if she could because of the screen door and the fact that Rory's voice kept raising with what she could only assume were incoming objections from James.

"Well, I'm not changing the venue. This wedding will take place in Oak Harbor, or it won't take place at all. Better yet, if it has to take place at St. Peter's, why don't you go ahead and marry your mother?"

There was another pause. Andrea moved over to the counter to finish mixing the batter. She could still hear her daughter moving back and forth.

"My grandmother is dying, James. I want her to be a part of this wedding, and the only way she'll get to do that is if it's kept here. I would have expected you to understand how important this is to me, to my family, but apparently, you don't...I gotta go...Bye."

Andrea looked around at her daughter the minute she heard the screen door close. "Morning, sweetie. How are you?"

"Hi, Mom," Rory greeted back, her voice low. She walked over to stand beside her mother, resting her hip against the counter as she stared at her mother's wrist, flicking back and forth as she whisked the batter.

"Sweetie, what's wrong?" Andrea asked, turning fully to face her daughter.

Rory tried to conjure a smile, but it failed miserably. She released a haggard breath and placed her hand on the counter before resting her head on it.

"Is it about the fight you had with James?"

Rory turned her head to stare wide-eyed at her mother.

"I didn't mean to pry, but the screen door was open, and I heard a bit of your conversation," Andrea confessed.

Rory straightened up, this time splaying her palms wide against the surface of the counter as she leaned forward. She closed her eyes and breathed in deeply before releasing it.

"Rory, what's going on?" Andrea reached across with her free hand to rest it on her daughter's upper arm encouragingly.

Rory turned to her, the distress in her green eyes telling. "His mother wants us to have the wedding in San Francisco at their parish church and the reception at Le Meridien because having it here doesn't fit with their image."

"What?" Andrea's eyes widened in surprise. "But that's ludicrous. Oak Harbor is a top spot for destination weddings, not to mention it's yours and James' choice entirely." Andrea couldn't help the way her voice rose with annoyance at James' mother's interference.

Andrea walked over to the stove and ignited it, then placed the griddle pan over the heat and added grease. "Sweetheart, listen to me," she started, turning to Rory, who was already staring back at her.

"This wedding should be about you and James celebrating the love that you both have for each other. Nothing and no one else should matter," she said with feeling.

There was a pause in the conversation as she reached for the pancake batter and began pouring perfect circles.

"It doesn't matter where it happens as long as it's what you both want. Even if you chose to elope, it's entirely your decision...but don't do that," she quickly tacked on, pointing the spatula in her daughter's direction for emphasis. This earned a small chuckle from Rory.

"I just wish James could understand where I'm coming from," Rory sighed. Andrea looked over her shoulder as she flipped the pancakes and nodded in understanding.

"Give it time, sweetie. You are two people from different worlds that chose to fall in love. What that means is that you have to work on nurturing this love, and that takes understanding and compromise, especially now that you'll be spending the rest of your life together."

"Yeah. I guess I didn't look at it that way."

Andrea turned to look at Rory. She could see the reservation in her daughter's eyes even though a smile ruffled her lips and her head bobbed in agreement.

"Are you sure there isn't anything else bothering you?" she prodded softly.

Rory's face clouded over, and it took her nearly a minute to answer. Plastering a reassuring smile on her lips, she replied, "Everything's okay, Mom. I was thinking about how busy it'll be when Jenny gets here."

"Jenny?" Andrea's face scrunched in confusion as she tried to determine if she knew the person.

"My wedding planner. She's coming a week before the wedding, so we can finalize everything," Rory explained.

"Oh...okay." Andrea turned back to the griddle, cracking the eggs, and shaking a reasonable amount of salt and pepper over them. Her eyes narrowed in thought, and she turned back to her daughter.

"But won't that be too late?" she reasoned.

"Um, no...not really," Rory replied. "Do you want some help?" she asked, gesturing to the remaining items on the counter.

"Thanks, sweetie. You can replace the filter in the coffee maker and add the beans," she instructed.

Rory reached for the coffee maker. Andrea turned back to the pan and started easing the eggs onto the waiting platter.

"Jenny's taking care of most of the heavy lifting. We've already decided on the theme, and she's already sourced the floral arrangements, the food and the band that'll be playing at the reception. We're getting the coroners."

Andrea inclined her head in her daughter's direction and smiled. "Isn't that the band you became obsessed with back in college?"

"Yup," Rory replied, popping the 'p.' A satisfied grin broke across her face. "I can't wait."

Andrea smiled, and some of the tension she'd felt from her daughter's obvious stress began to dissipate.

"Also, my friends will be coming in a few days early for my bridal shower. Marg said she's already booked the rooms for them and the groomsmen. James' parents and their guests will

A Spectacular Event

stay in town at the Candlewood Suites; it's more in keeping with their expectations."

A ping sounded, and Rory reached into her pocket to retrieve her phone. Andrea watched her carefully, noticing the deep furrowing of her brows as she stared at the screen.

"Everything okay?"

Rory looked up at her mother before staring at the phone once more. Pocketing the device, she plastered a smile on her lips and replied.

"Everything's fine."

"Okay," Andrea replied hesitantly.

"Want me to help set the table?" she asked, changing the conversation.

"Yeah, that would be great," Andrea replied.

"Thanks, Mom."

"For what?"

"For the talk." Rory smiled appreciatively at her mother, and Andrea returned the smile. She turned to finish plating the food.

Rory reached up to remove the breakfast dishes and headed for the dining room. Andrea turned to watch her go, a wave of concern washing over her. She was certain that Rory was keeping something back, something more disconcerting than just where the wedding was being held.

Chapter Six

Rory stretched her hands up, allowing her fingers to brush the headboard of her bed as she released a tired yawn. Her body ached all over. It would have been easy to accept that it was still dark out if not for the sliver of yellow light that streamed into the room and fell on her face from the slight shift in the heavy curtains covering the French window across from the bed. She struggled to lift her eyelids. They felt like they were secured in place with strips of adhesive, but she quickly closed them again— the brightness of the light was an offense to her irises, she released a low grunt. It felt like she'd been running a marathon instead of sleeping for the last eight hours. But then again, she hadn't gotten much sleep on account of her mind being flooded with questions about her and James and their future.

"*What about our wedding? Are your thoughts any clearer about us walking down that aisle come December 23?*"

James' question kept repeating in her mind. Were her thoughts any clearer? Was she sure that there would be an aisle to walk down come the time? No. she wasn't. It scared her. Just over a month and a half ago, she had been ecstatic, impatient even to become Mrs. James Davis. Now she was undecided. She couldn't help but wonder if this was a mistake. The fact that she couldn't voice her concerns to her mother or tell her everything that was currently happening with her, James, and his parents was a red flag to her.

Rory sighed as she thought about the situation deeper.

She knew without a doubt that she loved James, and she was confident that he loved her and wanted a future with her. What she also knew was how easily he caved to his parents' demands, especially Lenora's. She knew he hadn't wanted to work at his father's best friend's law firm as a corporate lawyer but had relented even though his passion was environmental law. It's the same way she knew he hadn't wanted to play lacrosse back in high school, but because his father had been captain of his lacrosse team and his father before him and so on, it had been expected of him, and so he fell in line. He loved to point out that he chose her over everyone his mother picked for him, but she wasn't sure that was enough. In every other way, it felt like he was choosing his parents, specifically his mother over her.

Her mother's words came back to her in that instant, *"You are two people from different worlds..."*

"The expectations that she grew up with in a single-parent home with a mother who struggled for more than half of her life to take care of her was at one end of the spectrum and those for James at the next end as he was born into wealth and protocol. It would definitely be difficult for him just to break away from it all at once.

However, the question remained unanswered in her mind. She didn't know if she still wanted to go through with the wedding.

Warm water flowed over Rory's head, flattening her ginger hair against her face as it cascaded down her body. She massaged her sore shoulders, sighing in relief as some of the tension eased away from her. A relieved sigh left her lips as she spent a few more minutes under the showerhead soaking up the warmth. After turning off the water, she stepped out of the shower and left the bathroom. After getting dressed, she headed downstairs.

The smell of bacon wafted to Rory's nostrils the moment she hit the bottom of the stairs. The sound of laughter floated to her ears the closer she got to the kitchen.

"Mmm. It smells great in here," Rory said appreciatively as she walked into the kitchen, where her family sat around the island enjoying breakfast.

"Good morning, Rory," her aunts greeted.

"Hi, honey," Andrea said, her face bright with a smile.

"Hi, Mom." She gave her mother a loving upper arm rub. "Hi, Grandma," she greeted the small woman that looked even frailer than when she'd arrived over a week ago. Becky simply smiled in acknowledgment. She walked over and bent to kiss her temple affectionately before taking a seat.

"How'd you sleep?" her mother asked as she helped herself to the bacon and eggs before swiping a bread roll from the basket.

"I slept well," Rory lied. "Where's Jules?" she asked, noticing that her cousin was missing.

"She wasn't feeling well," Cora expressed.

"Oh, okay." She turned her attention to her plate and took a bite of bacon.

"I'm going to dinner this evening,"

Rory looked across the table at her mother, surprised.

"Let me guess, with a certain Firefighter who can't seem to put the fire out that you've lit in his chest?" Jo smirked.

"Ha ha, very funny," Andrea deadpanned. "And yes, it is Donnie. He invited me to have dinner with him, his sons, and daughter-in-law. He wants us to get to know each other better.

Rory, you're invited too." Andrea turned expectant blue eyes on her daughter.

Rory's eyes widened in surprise as her aunts also turned to look at her. "Um…" She felt like a kid caught off guard by her teacher waiting on her to give a bright answer to their unexpected question even though she didn't raise her hand or ask to be put in that situation.

"Sure…okay," she agreed slowly.

Andrea, as if sensing her hesitance, went on to say, "It's fine if you don't want to come. You don't have to, sweetie."

"No, I do," Rory rushed out. "I want to come and be there for you, Mom. To support you." She also wanted to observe Donny and see how he treated her mother.

Andrea gave her an appreciative smile.

"Mom, do you need some help?"

Rory gaze moved to her grandmother, who seemed to be having a hard time moving the fork with food to her mouth. She stopped struggling and slowly lowered her fork to look up at the occupants at the table, her brown eyes filled with embarrassment.

"I…a-am…f-f-fi-ne." She lowered her gaze to the plate before her as her family stared helplessly back at her.

* * *

"Wow. You look…amazing."

Rory's lips curved into a smile as she watched the tall, blond firefighter greet her mother with stars in his eyes as he gazed at her.

"Thank you," Andrea returned demurely with a shy smile. "You look quite dashing yourself." She turned to Rory and beckoned with a slight nod for her to join her by the front door. "You remember my daughter, Rory," she said, moving to the side to reveal her fully.

"Of course," Donny responded. "Rory, it's nice to see you again. I'm glad you were able to join us this evening," he spoke with a genuine smile on his lips.

"Thanks. I'm honored to be joining you guys for dinner," she returned with a smile of her own.

Donny stepped to the side, revealing a young man with the same sandy blond hair only longer, nearly brushing the tops of his shoulders. He was tall, too— maybe just an inch shorter than Donny.

"This is my son, Trey," Donny introduced.

"Hi, Trey. It's nice to meet you," she greeted the young man, who also sported a slight scowl.

"Yeah. You too," he responded.

Rory drew back, surprised at his dry, uninterested tone. Donny glared at his son, who paid him no attention, and she looked over at her mother to see her with a small unsure smile.

"Hi, Trey. How are you?" she asked pleasantly.

"Hi. I'm fine, thanks," he replied, his voice dismissive. "Can we go now?" he asked, turning to his father, his gaze tight.

Donny gave the women an apologetic look before replying, "Shall we?"

Andrea reached out to take Donny's offered hand but quickly dropped it and shook her head *no* at the annoyed look from his son. Rory noticed the exchange. A surge of protectiveness overwhelmed her. Her mother had always been sure of herself and confident, but one look from Donny's son, and it felt like she was acting scared. She knew that it might take some time for Trey to warm up to her, but he was outright being mean to her mother, and she didn't like it.

The four walked silently to Donny's SUV and then entered it before it pulled out of the driveway. "Bruce and Janice are gonna meet us at the restaurant," Donny spoke into the silence.

He received a simple "Okay" from Andrea, who stared

ahead. Rory saw Donny release the steering and reach across the console to hold her mother's hand, intertwining their fingers. Her mother, in turn, squeezed his hand.

"So, Trey do you go to college here or back on the mainland?" she turned to ask the young man brooding across from her.

"Skagit Valley College."

"Oh, that's nice," Rory answered.

Trey simply grunted his replying and opted to turn his attention to the passing objects outside the moving vehicle. Rory took that as her cue to end her attempts at small talk with the moody young man.

The car pulled up to the restaurant. Donny got out and opened the door for both Andrea and Rory before handing the key to the valet. Rory took the time to admire the building's exterior. It was certainly ritzier than Willberry Eats with its sleek finish. The building was shaped like a boat with glass all-round displaying the interior that was lit by low-hanging lights. She could see the patrons inside enjoying their dinner and conversations. As open as it was, it still felt like she was looking in on their moments of intimacy.

"Welcome to Batten."

"Hi, we have a reservation under Hasgrove," Donny informed the smiling maître' d.

"Ah, yes. Here you are. Two members from your party have already arrived," he informed them. "This way, please," he directed, leading them to a table closer to the back where a woman and man were already seated.

"Dad, Andrea," the man happily greeted the minute they were standing before them.

"Hi, Bruce," Andrea greeted, smiling. She accepted the hug from the gentleman who also bore an uncanny resemblance to the older Hasgrove.

The woman was the next one to hug Andrea affectionately. "I'm happy you're here."

"Me too, Janice... you remember Rory?" she stepped aside to introduce her.

"Hi, Rory. It's nice to see you again," Janice greeted, her smile bright and genuine. Bruce shook her hand with a welcoming smile of his own.

"It's nice to see you again, too," Rory greeted back. "And congratulations," she said, looking down at her protruding tummy. "How far along are you?"

Janice looked down, too, before returning her gaze to Rory. "Thank you. Five months."

Donny gestured for them to take a seat, he and his sons taking their own seats after them.

Shortly after, their waiter, who introduced himself as Mark, came and took their orders before he was off again. They were offered complimentary wine, which they sipped, except for Janice, who got a mocktail, while they waited for their food to arrive.

Rory was enjoying her time with the Hasgroves, and she could see her mother was having a great time too. That made her happy. The conversation flowed, and so did the laughter. The only difficult part of their evening was the moody younger son, who sat glowering and creating awkward moments of silence when he refused to participate in the conversation.

"Why don't we go for a walk along the boardwalk? Maybe we could get some frozen dessert from the 'Sweet Treats' truck," Bruce suggested.

"That's a great idea, baby," Janice jumped up.

"Of course. You were on my mind when I thought of it," he replied with pride, pecking her lips affectionately.

Rory smiled at their interaction.

"Sure. Why not?" Andrea chimed in, smiling up at Donny, who inclined his head in agreement.

It was settled. They would take a stroll on the boardwalk along the inner harbor.

Bruce and Janice held hands, and Donny quickly joined his with Andrea, who gave him a nervous smile. He smiled encouragingly at her, and she visibly relaxed. Soon they were off, the couples in front, and Rory and Trey walking behind them.

"Hey, Trey. Can I talk to you for a bit?"

The young man looked over at her, his blue eyes wary and his mouth set in a grim line.

"I won't be long. I promise."

He looked at the retreating backs of the others before turning his gaze on her once more.

"Okay," he breathed out.

When Rory was sure the others were out of earshot, she turned and gave him a pointed look.

"Why do you dislike my mother so much?"

Chapter Seven

"I want to know what she has ever done for you to act like she is the worst person you've ever met," Rory pressed, waiting for Trey, whose eyes had widened in surprise at her question, to respond.

"I-I...I didn't say I didn't like her," he stammered.

"Oh yeah? Well, what do you call what you're doing? Hmm? You practically give her the stink eye every time she says something to you, or you see your father showing any kind of affection toward her. This whole dinner, you have been intolerable, so much so, that you affected the mood of everyone at the table," she listed, flailing her arms in frustration. "You're so hellbent on hating her that you're not even trying to give her a chance."

"I don't hate her," Trey exploded, catching her off-guard.

"Then why?" she returned passionately.

Trey, who had crossed his arms over his chest, allowed them to fall to his side as he released a heavy sigh. He walked over to the railing and looked out at the darkened water. Rory remained where she was, watching him. After some time, he turned back to her, the overhead lamp light illuminating his features enough for her to see his lips curled out dejectedly, his eyes downcast.

"I don't hate Andrea," he repeated. "I just didn't expect Dad to want to..." he trailed off and swallowed visibly before tilting his chin up until his eyes could connect with hers. Rory could see the vulnerability in their blue depths, or at least she thought it was. "I thought after my mom died that dad wouldn't get back into the dating ring, let alone look at another woman the way he used to look at Mom. He looks at Andrea just like he used to with Mom," he finished sadly.

Rory finally understood what was eating at him, but she also understood that she had an obligation to her mother to want what was best for her.

"I understand it's hard to see your father wanting to share his life with someone new after all that he had with your mother, Trey, but you have to allow your father the opportunity to be happy the way he wants to be. He's been through it all, and he's had enough time to grieve your mother," she spoke earnestly. "My mom has been through a lot, I know. I was there for most of it. So, believe me when I tell you that I am fiercely loyal to her."

Trey nodded his head in understanding and placed his hands in his pockets as he rocked on the balls of his feet.

"I know that you're the same with your father, and it comes out the way that I've witnessed. I'm happy for my mom that she's finally found someone who loves her and wants to make a future with her, but if this is going to hurt her because you can't accept her, then I would rather she not continue her relationship with Donny."

"That's not what I want." Trey pursed his lips and gave her an apologetic look. He released a heavy sigh. "Look, a part of the reason that I've been so difficult toward her is...because I like her...a lot. It feels like I'm betraying my mother's memory and I don't know...there's just this ball of emotions that has been flowing through me, and sometimes it comes out just the way you saw it tonight," he confessed.

"Everyone deserves to be happy, Trey. I'm pretty sure your mother would want to be happy even if it means accepting the love and care of someone who may end up in the role of a motherly figure to you," she reasoned. "Also, I'm pretty sure it would break both of our parents' hearts if they broke up."

"Yeah...I know," Trey nodded. "I'll try to do better and work on my emotions," he promised.

"Let's go catch up with the others before they eat all the dessert, and we get nothing."

Trey laughed in agreement as they hurried down the boardwalk to catch up with them.

"Hey, we missed you both," Donny greeted them when they finally caught up, his gaze questioning.

"Sorry about that, Dad. We needed some time away from you lovey-dovey couples before we had to gag from all the PDA," Trey responded with a smirk.

Donny turned to his son, his eyes wide, his jaw slack. Regaining his composure, he replied, "You'll get used to it, just like we'll have to get used to you and your girlfriend. By the way, when are you going to introduce us to her?"

"Oh, come on, Dad," Trey whined, embarrassed.

"Donny, stop. You're embarrassing him," Andrea advised. Donny held up his hands in surrender.

Trey cut his eyes to Andrea and gave her a small smile of thanks. Rory smiled at the progress, small as it might have seemed.

"So, what did you and Trey discuss when you were alone? I noticed he was awfully nicer when you both got back." Andrea turned to her daughter with a look of wonder as she removed her coat and put it in the small closet by the front door. "He's never been that civil to me, like ever," she finished in a nasal tone.

"Mom, first off," Rory chuckled and pointed at Andrea. "Never talk like that again, and secondly, I just told him that you are a wonderful person inside and out and that his father is lucky to have you in his corner."

"Oh, sweetie..." Andrea pulled her into a tight hug. "I love you so much."

Rory smiled. "I love you too."

Early the next morning, Rory went for a run. She jogged along the highway, enjoying the feel of the crisp morning air that nipped at her cheeks and washed over her as she ran perpendicular to it. She took the exit that led down to the seaside and came to a halt after running along the sandy shore for another fifteen minutes.

When her heart rate settled and her breathing evened out, Rory looked out across the horizon, marveling at the brilliant orange-red display of the rising sun breaking apart the dark monochrome sky. The rhythmic beating of the waves against the shore was calming, and her mind turned to James.

She missed him so much and wished he was there at that moment to experience the magnificence of nature's beauty. Instead, they were miles apart, and she didn't even know if he was as worried about the state of their relationship as she was. She wondered what he was doing now. With a heavy sigh, she turned and headed for home.

"Good morning, Aunt Cora. Have you seen Mom?" Rory snatched an apple from the fruit basket on the kitchen island and took a sizeable bite.

"Good morning, honey. Your mother went by the inn to help out for a few hours." Her aunt informed her. Cora returned to slicing the ham and cheese sandwiches she'd chosen to make for breakfast in halves.

"Okay, I'm gonna head over there."

"Don't you want to eat breakfast first?"

Rory eyed the sandwiches and felt her stomach grumble in agreement. "I'll take two of those," she pointed.

Cora removed the slices and placed them in a dish before sliding them over to Rory. "Coffee?"

"Yes, please," Rory responded.

After pouring her coffee, Cora placed the steaming hot mug before Rory. The rich aroma wafted to her nostrils and intoxicated her senses. Cora plated her own food and sat across from Rory.

"Where's everybody else?" Rory asked.

"Josephine is at the restaurant with Daniel, and Julia's still asleep. I'm gonna fix mom a plate when I'm done and take it to her."

"How is she?" Rory couldn't help the slight quiver in her voice as she asked.

Cora hesitated; fear flashed in her blue-gray eyes. "Mom is...hanging in there."

Rory didn't understand what her aunt meant but decided not to push further as it was evident the subject was upsetting.

"Everything will work out, Aunt Cora," she reassured her.

Cora reached across the island to rest her palm on top of Rory's hand gratefully. As soon as she was finished, Rory headed for the door and made her way to the inn.

Rory ran her palm over the colorful flowers and ornamentals that formed a wall on either side of the path, her fingers caressing the spiky, velvety, and rough exterior of each plant. The stunningly green lawn spread for as far as the eyes could search before ending in thick woodlands obscuring the view of the harbor. The view was truly magnificent, especially the inn. The three-story colonial-style white house was truly magnificent with its beautifully cut stone steps that led up to the wide front porch and the double French doors. The entire building was perpetuated by wide sliding windows and balconies that surrounded the upper floors.

Rory walked up the few steps and entered the foyer. Again, she paused to admire the open space with high ceilings that supported a chandelier just between the grand double staircase, the glass panels shimmering as they caught the morning light and cascaded like a waterfall. She loved everything about the building.

A painting on the wall caught her eye. Her feet moved on their own until she was standing before it, admiring the brush strokes and the warm use of colors that brought the art to life. She walked to the next piece that hung a few feet away. It was a painting of a little girl with wide, frightened eyes with a tear that was suspended on her cheek.

"You like it?"

Rory looked over her shoulder to see the smiling face of her mother.

"I love it," she replied, looking back at the painting.

"It was chosen by Marg," Andrea informed her. "She has a degree in event planning and design."

"She has impeccable taste," Rory complimented, earning another smile from her mother.

"Hear that, Marg? My daughter thinks you're awesome."

"I'm flattered," the woman responded, coming to stand with them as they stared at the painting some more.

"You have lovely taste," Rory turned to tell the woman sincerely.

"Thank you. I appreciate it," Marg responded. She then turned to face Rory. "Your mom says that you paint?"

"Um, a little," Rory replied shyly.

"She's a brilliant artist," Andrea jumped in.

"Maybe you could do a painting that we can hang in here," Marg suggested looking expectantly at her.

"Um...I'll think about it," she replied.

Marg gave her a warm smile.

"I'm sensing I missed something important here."

The three women turned to the gentleman looking at them quizzically.

"Hi, Ben," Andrea greeted warmly.

"Hi," came Marg's soft reply as she stared affectionately at him.

The group moved over to the reception area.

"I hope you don't mind, but I brought us lunch. Well, late brunch, actually," he said, looking at Marg. "You're welcome to join us," he turned to say to Andrea and Rory as if just remembering they were also there.

"No, that's fine. I'm sure you two lovebirds need your privacy," Andrea responded. "Rory and I will man the desk. Go..." Andrea made a shooing motion, ushering them out. Rory chuckled at her mother's antics.

The two spent the next hour at the desk before Rory decided to call it quits and head back to the main house. On her way back, she chose to walk the path that led to the back of the house. As she approached the back porch, she noticed Julia seated on one of the Adirondacks overlooking the harbor. Rory hesitated at the step and found herself walking over to her cousin.

"Hey, Jules," she greeted before she was upon her.

She noted that the girl reached up to swipe at her eyes. "Hi, Rory," she greeted back with slight smile.

"Are you okay, Jules?" Rory asked, staring in concern at her red, puffy eyes.

"I am. It's just pregnancy hormones making me emotional," she gave by way of explanation.

"Okay," Rory answered skeptically. She could tell that it was more than that. Something was definitely wrong. She pulled up one of the chairs and just sat beside her cousin, hoping to offer some comfort with her presence.

"My baby may not have a father," Julia revealed after some time.

Rory looked over at her but didn't say anything.

After more than a minute had elapsed, she started talking again. "He's in the army, and he's stationed overseas. I don't know where exactly, and I haven't been able to reach him. I tried contacting his family but none of the numbers I had worked. Finally, I got through to someone."

There was another long pause as Julia collected her thoughts. "She said she was his fiancé," she half whispered, her brows scrunching together as her eyes squinted as if still in disbelief. "I hung up pretty quick and haven't tried to reach out to them ever since." Jules sighed as a few errant tears escaped and rolled down her cheek.

She turned to Rory, the pain in her eyes tugging at her cousin's heart.

"I don't know what to do, Rory. Mom keeps asking me about what happened. Where is the father? I'm just too ashamed to tell her. I'm such a screw-up."

Rory reached over to hug her cousin as she sobbed uncontrollably. She could only imagine what Julia was going through.

Chapter Eight

"I ca-...I can't tell her...I just can't."

Rory rubbed her cousin's back soothingly like a caring mother as Julia's face remained pressed against her chest. Her tears had long soaked through Rory's blouse, causing it to stick to her skin, but she didn't mind. She was happy that she could offer some comfort to her cousin— something she'd never had the opportunity to do before. When she'd stopped sniffling, Rory removed her hands from around Julia, allowing her to raise her head to look at her.

"I don't know what to do," she spoke, fear causing her voice to shake.

"What about the father?"

"He doesn't factor in this...at least not anymore."

Sighing, Rory looked at her seriously. "Jules, I know it's hard, but I think you should tell him."

"No." Julia shook her head vehemently, her arms coming up to fold over her chest.

"It's the only fair thing to do," Rory pressed.

"Didn't you hear me say he has a fiancé?"

Rory turned from her cousin to look out at the crystalline blue waters a few meters from where they sat. The blue sky was riddled with fluffy white clouds, and the rock formations in the distance offered a serene atmosphere. The only thing was the conversation they were having was anything but calming.

"When Mom finally told me that I had a father, that he wasn't dead all along like she'd told me before, I was devasted. I felt betrayed..." Rory paused, choosing her words carefully. She turned to look at her cousin once more, her green eyes filled with regret. "I felt robbed, Jules. Of the choice to know my father, and as much as I understand why mom did it and I have forgiven her, it doesn't take away these feelings and what if questions."

Rory reached over and held her cousin's hand as she continued to speak. "It may not be the best option for you personally, but..." she squeezed Jules' hand. "You owe it to your child to give them and the father the option to get to know each other. Tell the father Jules. Let him decide what he wants to do with that news."

Julia's chest rose and fell as she folded her lips in on each other, and her brows came together in concern.

"Okay. I'll think about it," she spoke slowly.

"Tell your mother too. You'll need her in your corner more than anything."

Jules' eyes fluttered closed, and a gust of air escaped her lips.

Rory turned her attention back to the harbor.

"Thanks, Rory," Julia spoke after some time had passed.

"Oh, it was nothing," Rory brushed it off.

"I mean it," Jules replied with feeling. "I really needed someone to talk to. I used to be able to talk to my sister about anything, but Erin's been so busy, and it looks like she's battling her own crisis. I didn't want to burden her."

"In that case, you're welcome," Rory replied. The two

embraced, and Rory rose to her feet afterward, making her way toward the main house.

*　*　*

Rory stretched across the bed to reach her cell phone on the bedside table. The ringing stopped the minute she pressed the answer button and brought the device to her ear.

"Hello?"

"Are you trying to make my family the laughingstock of the century, or have you truly gone mad?"

"Lenora?" Rory asked, sitting up in a panic. She wished she'd looked at the caller id before answering.

"Of course, it's me. Who else could it have been?" The woman's acerbic tone caused Rory's skin to prickle with irritation. She rushed on. "Imagine my surprise when my son told me you weren't available to go shopping for a wedding dress because you were no longer in San Francisco and that you've jetted off to Oak Harbor instead. It has occurred to me that you must be planning to sabotage the wedding— to pull such a stunt only a month and a couple of days away from the wedding."

"That's not..." Rory paused, realizing that she was on the verge of losing her temper. Taking a deep breath through her nostrils, she slowly released it before continuing. "I'm sorry, Lenora, that was not my intention. I needed some time away to think about everything. James and I agreed it was fine for me to come to Oak Harbor to do just that. Also, you don't have to worry about the dress. My mom is going dress shopping with me."

Rory's steady breaths were the only thing she heard for almost half a minute as she waited for the woman to say something.

"You needed time to think," the woman finally said, her tone questioning. "What is there to think about? You're marrying one of the most eligible bachelors this side of the West Coast," she continued, matter-of-factly. "Any woman would be tripping over themselves to have him, but he chose you and yet...you're in Oak Harbor...thinking." Rory cringed at the disdain in her mother-in-law's tone as she said the last word.

"James' is fine with it. He understands," she reiterated, albeit more timidly than before.

Lenora pressed on as if she hadn't spoken. "On top of that, you want to have your wedding in that awful small town."

"It's no—"

"It isn't too late to change the venue back to our parish church. That's where it should have been, after all. You can always have your second wedding in Oak Harbor if you choose."

Rory had heard enough.

"Listen, Lenora. I am not some woman that James randomly chose to marry. I am his fiancé by choice because we have been together for more than three years, and we love each other. Whatever decision that will be made will be decided by both of us because this is a mutual partnership. Furthermore, I am not changing the venue. The wedding will be in Oak Harbor. You can either accept that or don't come at all."

"Well, I ne—" Lenora started, her voice full of indignation.

"I'm sorry, but I have to go now. I guess I'll see you at the wedding." Rory disconnected the call before the woman could get anything else out. Feeling drained physically and mentally, she decided to take a walk down to the dock after a quick shower.

Rory followed the pattern of the paved walkway with her eyes as her steps moved her toward the dock. There was a grass path to the left of the original path. It was a few meters away from where the thicket of trees bordering the property thinned to reveal the water and the reconstructed dock. Rory turned to look at the rustic-looking arbor covered by creepers decorated with flowering buds of varying shades. It was beautiful, and it led to an equally beautiful place, she was sure— her grandmother's flower garden, gifted to her by her husband, Rory's grandfather.

"I wish I got to know you, grandad," she breathed out, her lips pursed in sadness. She turned back to the straight path and continued toward the dock.

Rory walked across the wooden planks of the lower deck toward the boat moored there. She smiled at the words, **Silver Bullet** etched on the side, the varnish causing it to glisten. Her mother had told her it was a gift to her and her sisters from their father, the words' significance coming from their shared childhood experience. Rory kicked off her sandals and sat at the edge of the dock, her legs swinging back and forth as her toes grazed the water surface.

She looked out at the mountain ranges in the distance, ice capping a few of the rock faces that stretched to touch the blue skies. It was magnificent. Everything about Oak Harbor was magnificent— magical. How could she not choose to have her wedding here?

If only her mother-in-law wasn't such a meddlesome person who she was quite certain now despised her. She would definitely be having the wedding of her dreams. Not the one that she now had to accept where seventy-five percent of the guests were people she wouldn't know.

She wanted intimacy. No, she needed it. Even though she was just now building a relationship with them, her family meant a whole lot to her, and she wanted to be surrounded by them when she said her vows.

Fishing her phone out of her pocket, she dialed her fiancé.

James answered on the second ring.

"Hi," he breathed out, his tone relieved.

"Hi," she replied, her breath hitching. She missed him so much.

"Your mother called."

"What did she say?" he asked cautiously.

"She implied that I should be grateful that you chose me rather than all the rich socialites that would line up to marry you. It seems like they're a dime a dozen if you asked me."

James chuckled at her last statement and the sarcasm in her tone.

"You are one in seven billion, not easily replaced," he replied emphatically.

Her heart fluttered at his declaration, an involuntary smile breaking out on her lips.

Sobering up, she said, "Maybe you should try convincing your mother of that."

James sighed. "Rory, I love you. I only want to marry you. Why can't that be enough?"

Her grip on her phone loosened. She placed her other hand along the edge to keep it in place as she replied. "It can't," she whispered.

"Why not?" James pressed.

Pain seared through her heart. *How could he not understand it?*

"Your mother has interfered with our relationship from the very beginning, James. She doesn't like me; it makes no sense for you to try to convince me otherwise, and I know you try to protect me from her but only to a point because you also don't want to hurt her feelings."

"Rory," he sighed, the tiredness in his voice palpable.

"Let me finish. Please?" she begged.

His silence encouraged her to speak. "You wanting to marry me can't be enough because I'm not sure how far you're willing to go to protect me from your mother if it comes to that. That's not something that I should have to worry about, James." She paused to look at the pristine water below, the tiny ripples moving the boat back and forth gently. "Your mother has been trying to derail our wedding, and I would be lying if I said I didn't resent her for it. The concerning thing is that I think..." Rory took in a gulp of air.

"I think I'm starting to resent you too because it feels like you've left me to fight this battle all on my own, and I am bound to lose...I love you, but right now, it's not enough."

Rory waited for him to speak, her heart pounding against her chest in anticipation. She'd been more candid about the Lenora situation than she ever thought she could be.

"Where does that leave us then?" he finally asked, his voice flat.

Rory sighed. "I need you to tell your mother to back off. She needs to stop meddling in our plans. I will include her in the things I'm okay with including her in. I will not be strongarmed into it. I need you to let her know that. My mom is going to take me shopping for a dress in Seattle, my cousin Kerry is baking the cake, and I found a wonderful florist to help with the arrangements. Jenny is taking care of everything else."

"Okay. If I do all that you've asked, will that be confirmation enough that the wedding will go on?"

Rory thought about the question. She hesitated for a bit, not sure what to tell the man waiting for her response. She wasn't sure if that would be enough. She breathed out and then responded.

"We'll see."

Chapter Nine

"If anything happens while we're away, don't hesitate to call."

"Relax, Cora. Everything will be okay." Jo smiled reassuringly.

"But—"

"Relax, sis. Jo is perfectly capable of looking after mom," Andrea jumped in, realizing Cora was trying to find a way to stay back out of worry for their mother. But she needed this trip to Seattle just as much as the others. "Besides, nothing is going to happen."

Cora released a heavy sigh. "You're probably right," she relented.

"Everyone ready to go?"

Andrea looked up at her daughter standing at the top of the stairs with Julia. A broad smile graced her lips as warmth spread through her. She was going wedding dress shopping with her daughter just like she'd imagined since the first day she held her in her arms and vowed that she would never miss any of the special moments in her life.

"Yeah, sweetie. We were just going over a few things with Jo," she replied as the two descended the stairs to join them.

Andrea turned for the front door, and the others did the same. Five minutes later, they were bundled into Cora's olive-green land rover. For another twenty-five minutes, they were driving past the Whidbey welcome sign and making their way onto the Deception Pass bridge before transitioning onto the state highway as they made their way to Seattle.

"Okay. So, I've booked fitting appointments with two bridal shops. I did my research, and their reviews were great. I'm hoping you'll find the wedding gown of your dreams," Andrea turned in her seat to inform Rory, who sat in the back with Julia.

"Me too," Rory smiled, hopeful.

"Where to?" Cora asked from the driver's seat.

"Issaquah, we're going to Gilman Village," Andrea instructed.

Cora inputted the information into the GPS. A half-hour later, they arrived at their destination. After parking in the designated parking spot, they all got out of the car, taking in their surroundings.

"This looks so cool," Rory breathed out, awestruck.

Andrea smiled. True to its name, Gilman Village was the picture of a small town. The stores were at one-time homes, barns, and farmsteads and had been converted and renovated into shops. It felt like a scene out of an old western where the town's buildings were stacked up against each other on either side of a dirt road. Only the pathways in the village were paved roads and canopied, wooden walkways.

"We're going to shop number twenty-seven."

The group followed Andrea. A few minutes later, they were standing on the outside of the bridal boutique. The large four paneled French windows gave them a clear view of the beautiful white gowns on display. She pushed open the door leading the others inside.

"Hello, welcome to Imperial fit," a short woman with a bubbly smile greeted. "My name is Gloria."

"Hi, Gloria, I'm Andrea," Andrea greeted back. "I made an appointment for Aurora Hamilton," Andrea informed the woman.

"Oh yes. We were expecting you," the woman replied before looking behind her to the others. "And which of you lovely ladies are the bride to be?"

"Um, I am," Rory responded, raising her hand halfway.

"Congratulations are in order for you then," the woman responded, the smile never slipping from her face. "If you will all follow me, I've already set up a room for your fitting. Lydia will personally be helping you to find the dress of your dreams."

Just then, a tall brunette appeared, a bright smile on her lips. "Hi, I'm Lydia," she introduced herself.

After the introductions had ended, Lydia directed them to one of two doors at the back of the main store. It opened into a large, private dressing room.

The room was large and decorated with a plush white sofa and matching armchairs. A dressing room at the back, a raised platform, and three floor-length mirrors completed the room's décor. Andrea scanned the room in appreciation, as did the others.

"Would you ladies like some refreshment?" Lydia asked as she wheeled a service tray into the room.

The women each accepted the glass of orange juice offered before taking seats on the comfortable pieces of furniture.

Another attendant brought in a long rack of wedding dresses and left.

"So, what are you looking for your dress to be or not?"

Lydia asked, hands clasped above her chest as she looked at Rory.

"I'm. not. Sure?" Rory looked over at her mother for help.

Andrea sprang into action. "What are your suggestions?" she directed at the attendant.

Lydia looked over at Rory. "Could you stand for a bit please and..." Her index finger rounded to indicate that she wanted Rory to spin.

Rory rose to her feet and did as instructed, twirling in slow motion.

"Thank you," Lydia expressed. Rory sank back into the plush couch.

"A ball gown would probably be the most fitting for you. Firstly, it's the most traditional look and would be very flattering to your shape with its full flare skirt making your hips look wide. Or a mermaid gown. It fits close at the bodice down to the thighs then flares at the knees, but it gives the illusion of being taller than you actually are."

The woman stepped over to the rack, sliding the hangers across the metal rod.

"Here we go," she spoke triumphantly, turning to reveal a ball gown with a sweetheart neckline, the entire bodice completed with sequins.

"Let's start off with this one," Lydia suggested, holding the gown out to Rory.

"Okay." Rory accepted the dress and headed for the changing room. "Mom, can you help me?"

"Of course, sweetie," Andrea replied, following her into the changing room. Ten minutes later, they emerged.

"What do you think?" she asked, twirling.

The bodice hugged Rory's chest before flaring out from the waist. The dress was very lovely and fit her well. Still, Andrea didn't like it, and it was evident that Rory wasn't fond of the dress either.

"Why don't you have a look in the mirror first, then you can decide," Julia suggested.

Rory lifted the hem of the dress and walked over to the mirror. She stood before her reflection, contemplating. Finally, she turned to make her decision.

"Uh-uh," she shook her head. "I don't think this will work." Andrea nodded in agreement.

"No worries. We do have other options," Lydia replied reassuringly. She pulled another dress from the rack. Rory took it and headed for the changing room with Andrea in tow once more.

When she emerged from the room, the expectant faces fell, a clear indication they didn't like it. Rory went before the mirror. Her lips dipped into a deep frown.

"You don't like it," Lydia concluded the moment Rory turned around.

"I'm sorry, it's just..."

"You don't have to apologize," the woman stopped her. "I always tell my clients that shopping for the perfect dress is usually the hardest part of the wedding preparations."

"That is so true," Cora chimed in. "I remember shopping for my own dress all those years ago. I almost cried."

"You never told me that. How come?" Julia folded her arms over her protruding tummy and stared at her mother.

"I must have visited five different bridal boutiques trying to find the perfect dress, then I found it, but someone beat me to it. I literally broke down in the middle of the room."

"I remember," Andrea snorted. "You should have seen your mother, Jules; you'd have thought the world was coming to an end."

"Hey," Cora called out, offended. "It wasn't that bad," she pouted.

Andrea turned to her niece, mischief twinkling in her eyes.

"Your mother wouldn't leave the bridal shop until the other bride decided to give her the dress."

"She gave it up because she had another choice that she wanted more, and me wanting that specific dress pushed her to go get it."

"I would have loved to see you that day, so totally out of control," Julia mused.

"You wouldn't have," Cora returned. Her daughter smiled wryly.

Rory tried on two other dresses, but none of them gave her the desired look she was searching for.

"I'm sorry we couldn't be of more assistance to you, Ms. Hamilton. We do hope you will find the perfect dress." Gloria smiled warmly.

"I'm sorry, too," Rory responded with a sheepish smile.

"Okay, where are we going now?" Cora asked.

"Ballard Avenue," Andrea replied.

Cora nodded and backed the car out of the parking lot before setting course for their destination. A half-hour later, they were entering Bridal Bliss Boutique.

Rory sighed defeatedly.

"What's wrong?" Andrea asked her as she zipped up the back of the fifth dress she was trying since they arrived.

"I'm just...frustrated and...disappointed," Rory breathed out, hanging her head.

Andrea reached up to rub her daughter's shoulder blades comfortingly. "We'll find the perfect dress, even if it takes the whole day and visiting every bridal boutique in the continental US," Andrea promised.

Rory reached up to rest her right hand over her mother's hand on her left shoulder. "Thanks, Mom."

Andrea placed a kiss against her daughter's cheek before turning her around. "Let's go see what this dress is about," she instructed. Gathering the train in her hands, she allowed her daughter to walk out with her in tow.

When Rory was situated in front of all three mirrors, Andrea released the train and smoothed it out behind her. Cora and Julia came to stand behind them.

Andrea's hands went to her mouth as her eyes glistened. Rory stood immobile; her mouth opened in surprise. "This is the one," she breathed out the moment she recovered from her stupor.

What made the dress most spectacular than the others she'd tried was the delicate floral lace detail that circled her neck before traveling down her arms and over the bodice. It looked as if it was floating along her body before transitioning into a seamlessly contoured skirt with floral motifs along the hem and forming the train of the dress.

"Yes, it is," Andrea affirmed. "You look so beautiful," she smiled, catching her daughter's eyes in the mirror. Rory gave her mother a watery smile.

"You look really beautiful, Rory," Julia complimented.

"Oh my god! Does she ever," Cora agreed.

"Have we come to a decision?" the attendant came to ask, her voice full of hope.

Rory turned to the woman, a broad smile on her lips.

"We're taking this one."

"Excellent," the woman clapped.

After final measurements were taken, the owner promised them that the dress would be altered as per the specifications and shipped by the first week of December.

The four women left the boutique all smiles. After stopping by Chick-fil-A for lunch, they headed back to Oak Harbor.

"I want to stop by Kerry's bakery. I need to make the final decision on the flavor and icing finish," Rory informed them.

An hour and a half later, they pulled up to **'Heavenly Treats'** in bold confetti colors.

"Hi, guys. I wasn't expecting to see you here. Is everything okay?" Kerry greeted them the moment they walked through the door.

"Everything's fine," Cora assured their cousin, hugging her.

"Yeah," Andrea confirmed, hugging her.

"I wanted to go over the cake samples," Rory spoke up.

Kerry looked over at her in surprise. "Wow, that's sudden," she voiced. "Good thing I'm always prepared," she smiled. "Hi, Jules. How are you?"

"Hi. I'm okay," Julia answered with a small wave.

"And how's the little munchkin?" She averted her attention to her belly.

"Baby's fine," Julia replied with a tight smile.

Noting the tension in the room, Andrea spoke up. "So, Kerry, you said you have samples?"

"Yeah. Let me get them. I would have invited you all-around back, but you know health and safety protocols and all."

"That's fine," Andrea assured her.

Rory disappeared into the kitchen, returning five minutes later with a dish with cake samples. Rory tasted as per Kerry's instructions.

"I think I'm going to go with the chocolate and lemon," Rory decided.

"Great. Excellent choices," Kerry commended. "Have you hired a caterer for the event yet?"

"Um...no?"

"Well, I know the perfect catering company. They're very professional and reasonable too."

"Okay. I'll have to discuss it with James, but you can give me their number so I can share it with him and Jenny, my wedding planner."

"Sure thing," Kerry agreed. "So, guys, I was thinking that for our next family get-together, we should maybe do something away from the house," she suggested.

"That's a good idea," Andrea agreed.

"What were you thinking?" Cora asked, equally interested.

"A beach picnic at Double Bluff Beach."

"I'm in," Andrea agreed.

"Me too," came Cora's answer.

"What about you two?" Kerry asked, looking over at Rory and Julia. When they hesitated to reply, she added. "Relax. There will be other young people your age there."

"I'm in," they replied simultaneously.

Chapter Ten

"Mmm, breakfast is wreaking havoc on my senses. I feel so full, and I haven't even had any yet," Rory said the minute she stepped into the kitchen.

"Good morning, Sweetie," her aunt Jo who stood by the stove with a spatula in hand, gave her a smile over her shoulder.

"Good morning, Aunt Jo," she replied. "Everything looks and smells really good," she complimented, looking at the spread before her. A platter of eggs, freshly baked biscuits, cinnamon rolls in a basket cooling, cooked sausages and bacon, French toast, and fruit filled the tabletop. Rory doubted anything else would hold on there. She could also smell the deep dark roast percolating.

"You really are an amazing chef. I haven't tasted anything, and I'm already salivating."

"Thanks, sweetie," Jo returned with a smile.

Just then, the others came filing into the kitchen. "You truly outdid yourself today, Jo. Everything looks good," Andrea complimented.

"When has it never?" Jo turned to look at her sister, eyes narrowed.

"Told you she'd go off," Andrea laughed, turning to Cora was assisting their mother to her seat around the kitchen island. "That's ten bucks."

"You're so annoying, Drea," Jo huffed, earning more laughter from the others.

"And you're too easy to rile up," Andrea replied between laughs.

"Whatever," Jo muttered. Ignoring her sister, she turned to their mother. "Hi, Mom," she smiled softly.

"H-h-...hi, hon-n-ney," Becky replied, stopping to catch her breath and plastering on a smile.

Rory noted the worried looks the sisters exchanged, her own heart filling with dread. Becky had been finding it extremely difficult to speak. In most instances, she had only been able to say one full sentence before she had to stop to catch her breath. She noticed that her grandmother had also become reserved, opting to spend more time in her room under the guise of being too tired. Rory knew, like the others, that it was more than that. It pained her heart to see her like that.

She hoped their trip to Double Bluff would raise her grandmother's mood a bit, even if only for a day.

"All right let's eat. We don't have the entire day to do so. We have to be out of here within the hour if we want to beat the morning sun," Cora advised.

"Hi, grandma," Rory greeted, kissing her grandmother's cheek. Beck slowly raised her hand to caress the side of her face. Rory leaned into it, enjoying the affection. Becky's hand dropped, and she took her seat.

"I made fresh orange juice," Josephine announced, going over to the refrigerator to remove the jug and coming to take a seat around the island as well.

"Rory..."

She looked over at her aunt, waiting for her to continue.

"Would you like to say grace?" she asked.

"Um, sure," she accepted. After indicating that they should hold hands, she started. "Dear Lord, thank you for this meal that we are about to eat, thank you for this family and thank you for love. Amen."

"Amen," the others repeated. They dug into the food happily.

"So, Rory, have you decided on the menu for the reception?"

"No. Not yet," Rory answered her aunt. "I'm still waiting for the list from his side of the family to work from," she explained.

Josephine's brows furrowed in thought. "Can I make a suggestion?" she asked.

"Shoot," Rory directed.

"Work with what you have currently. That way, you will give the caterers ample time to start making their preparations, and you can add and take away as you go. If you wait until the last minute to get this done, things may turn out a lot different than you anticipate," she suggested.

Rory nodded her understanding.

"Have you decided to use the caterers Kerry suggested?"

"Yes. I discussed it with James, and he's all for it. I turned their number over to Jenny too."

"That's good," Josephine said, nodding her approval.

"I was also thinking for the ceremony itself to not be so traditional and not have it at the church," she revealed.

"Where would you have it then?" Andrea turned to her daughter to ask, her eyes registering concern.

"I was thinking about maybe having it here by the dock or by the lawn behind the inn, using the gazebo as the altar," she suggested.

"That's a wonderful idea, Rory," her mother encouraged.

"That way, you can have both the wedding and the reception in the same location."

Rory nodded yes.

After breakfast, the women packed into Cora's SUV and Andrea's Jeep and made their way to Double Bluff beach to have a day of fun with the extended family.

They met up with the others at the parking lot. After removing their things from the backs of the cars, they walked over to the grassy area with picnic benches and a barbecue, already fixtures around the area. A family of four was already occupying one of the picnic benches, but there were enough to host them.

"Rory!"

Rory turned around to see her mother standing with a young woman and a young man waving her over.

Placing the igloo on the tabletop, she sauntered over to them.

"Sweetie, this is Natalie and Jordan, Rhonda's children," Andrea introduced. "You didn't meet them because they didn't get to come to the funeral..."

"We were in England visiting our father's parents," Natalie, who looked to be the younger of the two, explained.

"Okay. Well, it's nice to meet you both," she replied, holding her hand out to them. "I'm always happy to meet the rest of my family, considering I didn't get that chance before." She saw her mother visibly shrink back and wished she had chosen her words more carefully.

"I'm very happy to meet you, too," Jordan said with a smile as he shook her hand.

"Your mom said you're getting married?"

"Yes, that's correct," Rory answered the young woman, a small smile on her lips.

"Congratulations."

"Thank you."

"Looks like you can take the Hamilton family out of the barbecue, but you can't take the barbecue out of the Hamiltons," Jordan laughed, looking behind them.

Rory turned to see what he was looking at. A broad grin appeared on her lips at the sight. Uncle Luke stood by the old rusty barbecue grill adding wood chips to its hearth. Andrea burst into laughter and Rory joined her shortly after.

"There will always be a barbecue as long as Uncle Luke is involved," Andrea spoke.

"Well, while he tries to get that old crust bucket to work, I think I'm gonna head down to the beach," Natalie spoke. Jordan nodded.

"What about you, Rory?" the young woman turned hopeful brown eyes in her direction.

"I want to take a dip but not just yet," she answered.

"Okay."

"So, is Donny coming?" Rory turned to ask her mother after Natalie and Ben left.

"No, he had to work today," Andrea sighed.

Rory smiled at how obvious it was that her mother missed the man she was falling in love with. It was cute. It reminded her of how sad she would get when James couldn't go with her to every function she had to attend and when he had to go to corporate conferences, leaving her at home by herself. Everything was changing. Here she was, miles away from him, missing him terribly but also not sure that she actually wanted to see him. This was the most confused she had ever been.

"Hi, guys. Sorry we're late."

Rory looked behind her to see Ben and Marg walking in their direction, Ben's nineteen-year-old son Josh behind them.

"Hey, Ben. Hi, Marg, Josh," Andrea greeted, hugging the two older adults.

"Hi, Drea, Rory," Marg greeted back.

"We actually got here a half hour ago, so you didn't miss anything," Andrea explained to them.

"Hey, cuz," Josh greeted Rory with a smile.

"Hey, Josh," she greeted back. "Where's your sister?"

"At home freaking out about wanting to miss the deadline to submit her thesis," he replied, rolling his eyes.

Rory chuckled. "I know the feeling," she empathized.

"Well, I don't but what I can say is that she has been driving me up the wall," he spoke in annoyance.

"You know you love her," Rory teased.

A small smile creased his lips. "I do."

Another half hour later, Rory had greeted all the members of her family who'd attended the trip.

She decided to head down to the beach where the younger population had begun congregating. Reaching for her jean shorts, she quickly pulled them over her bikini bottom before removing the floral print dress she'd worn.

"Mind if I join?" she called out to her cousins playing beach volleyball.

"Yeah, of course," Dianne accepted. "You can join Nikki's side, even out the numbers," she instructed.

Rory set in position and waited for the opposing side to serve the ball. She sprang into action the second the ball left Natalie's hand and headed over the net. Rushing up, she hit the ball to Nikki, who skillfully got it over the net; however, the volley continued for another fifteen seconds before Josh hit the ball too low for anyone on Rory's team to reach it. They screamed in jubilation at the win.

"Rory, you serve," Nikki instructed.

She nodded and accepted the ball. Throwing it into the air, she jumped, flicking her wrist as her palm connected to the ball and sent it over the net. The speed of the serve proved too much for Dianne's side, and the point went to them. They rejoiced in like fashion.

The game continued for another forty-five minutes, the group opting for a time out to get refreshment.

"Hey, Jules," Rory greeted her cousin, sitting on one of the picnic tables facing the beach.

Julia looked up with a half-smile.

"Are you all right?" Rory asked in concern.

"I am," she replied simply.

After donning the lemonade, Rory sat down beside her and looked out at the water, the waves lightly crashing against the shore. She could also see the mountain range in the distance. A bird hovering in the distance dived nose first into the water and dipped up to the sky almost instantaneously.

"Tell you what, why don't we lay our towels on the sand and lie down...take in some sun and maybe a dip?" she suggested, figuring that Julia was feeling left out.

"I d—"

"Come on, Jules. It'll be fun." She turned and gave her cousin puppy eyes.

"All right. Fine," Julia chuckled.

The two got their towels and sunscreen and marched down to the shore. They sat cross-legged on the towels and continued to stare out at the ocean.

"Mind if we join you?"

Rory looked up to see Dianne and Nikki.

"Yeah. Of course," she replied.

The women spread out their towels before situating themselves.

"Let me help you with that." Rory stretched her hand out to accept the tube Julia held.

Rory squeezed a generous amount of the slick cream into her palms before rubbing it over her cousin's back. "Can I?" she asked, looking at Julia's belly.

"Sure," Julia permitted.

Rory rubbed the cream over the stretched skin, marveling at

the complexity of the female body. She felt a slight flutter against her palm. She looked up at Julia, surprised.

"The baby just kicked," Julia confirmed.

Rory looked back at her cousin's tummy in wonder.

"Here, touch here."

Surely enough, Rory felt the same slight pressure against her hand where Rory placed it.

"This is so amazing," she spoke in admiration.

Julia smiled knowingly.

Rory turned her attention to the other two women. "So, Dianne, when is the wedding?" she asked her cousin, who was sporting a beautiful piece on her ring finger.

"Derek and I haven't set the date just yet, but we hope to do so soon," Dianne replied, lightly spinning the ring on her finger. "I can't wait to be Mrs. Calloway," she added, gushing.

"That's wonderful," she replied. Rory felt her stomach dip. She turned to look out at the horizon, feeling anything but joy and only the turmoil of her own situation.

Chapter Eleven

Rory sighed for the third time since returning from Double Bluff. Her mind had been on James the whole afternoon after witnessing how happy and in love Dianne was. Every time she'd spoken of her fiancé, her face brightened, and her eyes twinkled. Rory wouldn't say she was jealous of her cousin, but the fact that she and James were in a rocky place made Dianne's overzealous sharing too much.

As she stared out across the porch rails sunbathing, everything in its path had a warm orange glow as the sun began its descent over the horizon. She wondered what James was doing at this moment.

She reached for her phone on the low table and speed dialed her fiancé before raising the phone to her ear. She needed to hear him. She needed him to tell her that they would be okay. The phone rang until his voicemail message came on. With another heavy sigh, she disconnected the call. She stood to her feet and went inside. En route to the stairs, she heard sounds coming from the living room. Abandoning her original plan, she went to investigate. She found her grandmother propped up by pillows behind her on the couch, her feet resting on the ottoman, her eyes trained on the television playing Law and Order.

"Hey, grandma," she greeted, calling the woman's attention to her presence.

"Hi, sweetie. Are you ok—ay?"

"I am," Rory assured her, smiling warmly.

"How are you feeling?"

Becky's lips pursed, her eyes taking on a faraway look. Rory went to sit by her, resting her hand on top of the one in her lap. "It's fine. You don't have to say anything, I understand," she spoke reassuringly.

Becky gave her a tight-lipped smile, her brown eyes filling with pain and regret before she looked away. "H-how is y-your yo-young m-a-n?" she stuttered, turning her eyes back on her.

It was Rory's time to look away. "To tell you the truth, Grandma. I don't know," she answered truthfully. Her shoulders fell, and she stared at the thick multicolored carpet covering the wooden floor. "I haven't a clue, and the sad part is it's been more than a month that I haven't been able to confidently answer that question," she continued to say, letting the truth spill that they were having problems in not so many words.

Becky flipped her palm to give Rory's hand a squeeze in support. Her hand was stiff, and not much pressure was applied, but Rory smiled over at her grandmother, appreciating her attempt at comfort.

"I a-am s-so-sorry y-ou are going through th-this. I w-wi-wish th-there was some-th-thing I c-c-could do to ma-ma-make y-you feeeel better."

"This is enough, Grandma," Rory replied, raising their connected hands. "I'm just glad I can talk to you."

"U-un-t-til I can-n-not a-any-"

"I'm happy for the now." Rory gave her a grateful smile, leaning against her.

A warm smile broke out on Becky's lips.

"Dinner time."

Rory looked up to see her mother in the doorway staring at them curiously.

"Okay, thanks, Mom. I'll take grandma."

Andrea inclined her head in acknowledgment before moving away from the door.

Rory rose up and extended her hand to Becky. The woman reached forward, grasping Rory's forearm to propel herself forward. Rory placed her free hand under her grandmother's elbow and eased her into a standing position before tucking her hand in the crook of her bent arm. Slowly they made their way to the dining room, Becky dragging her left leg.

After dinner, Rory made her way upstairs to take a long hot shower before falling into bed physically and emotionally exhausted.

"Ha ha, you don't have a father. You can't come to the father-daughter dance because you don't have a father."

Tears flowed freely down Rory's face as she stood frozen in the center of the ring the other children formed around her on the playing ground as they mocked her.

"You don't have a father; you don't have a father."

Feeling helpless, she stuck her thumb into her mouth, and her heart pounded in her chest. Who knew second graders could be so mean? Her mother had told her when she'd complained that her classmates were mocking her, she'd told her not to listen to them. "You are perfect just the way you are. A father doesn't make you special. You are special because you have a heart of gold. If you ignore them, they'll stop."

But they didn't. It only got worse and made her miss the father she'd never met. A father she'd been told was dead.

"You don't have a father! You don't have a father! No one will ever love you! They all leave you!"

The chants got louder and louder, beating against her ear drums.

Her mother had said she was complete even with the absence of her father. She had all the love she'd ever need from her, and someday her Prince Charming would sweep her off her feet and shower her with the love the way she deserved.

However, at that moment, her chest felt hollow. Something was missing. She wished what the children were chanting wasn't true. She wished she had a father to show up and shut them up. They would take to the dance floor, and he would hold her by the hand and twirl her and lift her to his chest and sway with her. He would then tell her that she was his little princess and that he loved her very much and would never ever leave her again. How she wished that were true.

Suddenly the setting changed. Rory found herself standing at the end of a very long aisle in her wedding gown. James and the priest stood at the other end. Just then, she felt her hand being hooked in the crook of an arm. She looked up to see a faceless man. The wedding march began. She tore her eyes away from him to focus on her fiancé, smiling at her encouragingly.

A smile graced her lips, but inside she felt queasy. Something wasn't right. Still, she was willing to ignore it, to press forward and marry the man of her dreams. The faceless man took a step forward, indicating that they should start moving. She looked out at the faces of their witnesses on either side of the aisle. Some faces, namely her family and friends, smiled and cheered while the others stared at her, their stares completely unfiltered and filled with disdain. She turned her attention back to the altar.

As she moved forward, the feeling in her chest became more pronounced. Her feet also started to feel heavy, and the dress felt too tight. Any minute now, she would faint. Beads of sweat appeared at her temple. Soon she realized that she had been walking for some time but couldn't reach the altar. She wanted to call out to James for him to meet her halfway but decided against it.

When she finally started to make progress, James' smiling face began to blur. She looked up at the faceless man in concern, but he didn't turn to look at her, only tugged her forward. Rory turned back to the altar, full-out sweating. James' face had disappeared completely. Her lips parted in horror as his body disappeared as well, to be replaced by his mother, a triumphant smirk on her lips.

Rory tugged at her arm, wanting to release herself from the faceless man, but his hold only tightened as he dragged her toward her mother-in-law.

"Did you honestly think that I would stand by and allow this farce of a wedding to take place?" Lenora sneered down at her when the man deposited her at the bottom step of the raised platform.

Rory was dumbstruck. She felt just as helpless as she'd felt back in elementary school. Her ears rang, her heart fought to leave her chest, and she was sweating bullets. She fought the urge to raise her hand and stick her thumb in her mouth.

"After all that I have invested in my son for you to come and ruin that..." the woman shook her head horrifically. She turned back to Rory, the smirk returning to her lips.

"Lenora, you can't do this. James lo—"

"He doesn't love you!" the woman shouted, her eyes firing up like angry coals.

"You bewitched my son, but now he's coming to his senses. He sees that you have nothing to offer him." The woman released a sinister laugh. "Can you imagine? Him with a mere kindergarten teacher, the heir of the Davis fortune. Ludicrous."

Rory felt tears prick the corners of her eyes as she turned and frantically searched through the faces in the pew, trying to find

James. Instead, accusatory eyes stared back at her as the people became a collective body of accusers.

"Lenora...please. Where is James? I need to talk to him," Rory pleaded, the tears breaking free. Black tears ran down her cheeks.

"Where is James? Where is James?" the woman asked mockingly, a salacious grin on her lips.

"James isn't here. He was never going to be at the altar waiting for you."

"Why are you doing this?" cried gutturally.

Lenora fixed Rory with a sinister stare. "I thought it was obvious that I made myself clear," Lenora replied calmly. "You do not belong in our world. You are not good enough for James—"

"I am good enough. I am special," Rory cried.

"Who told you that? Your mother?" Lenora scoffed. She fixed Rory with a serious glare. "You. Are. Not. Special. You're...ordinary. James deserves extraordinary."

The woman folded her arms over her chest and looked at Rory with what she could only term as sympathy. "That's the same reason why your father didn't want you. You're just...ordinary."

Rory staggered. The woman's words delivered a heavy blow to her chest.

"Think about it...he had a whole other family. Children that he actually wanted, while your mother had to work hard just to make ends meet. Not once did he think about you, wonder how you were living, if you were alive or dead."

"Stop talking," Rory managed to get through her blocked airway. She put her hands over her ears, trying to get away from the words Lenora spoke— from the truth.

"Your father didn't love you, and neither does James."

"Shut up! Shut up!" Rory screamed, her black, runny tears

splashing onto her wedding dress, leaving a trail of damage to the delicate fabric where it landed.

"James loves me. I know he does," she reasoned, not sure if she was trying to convince Lenora or herself.

Her mother-in-law laughed maniacally.

"He doesn't love you. How could he?" she jeered.

"He loves me," Rory affirmed.

"If he truly loves you, where is he? Not in this church and certainly not in Oak Harbor fighting for you," she said matter-of-factly.

Rory glanced around the church once more, but it was useless. She already knew he wasn't there. Her tears continued to fall, and her heart sank to the bottom of her chest, leaving the space hollow.

"Your wedding was destined to be like this all along," Lenora smiled victoriously. "Groom less."

Suddenly there was a crescendo of mocking laughter from behind her. Rory couldn't take it. She crouched down with her hands over her ears as the laughter got louder, drowning out everything else.

Rory woke with a start, her hand flying to her chest as her heart beat wildly against her ribcage. Sweat covered her forehead and arms.

"What was the hell?"

Chapter Twelve

Andrea placed her sneaker-clad foot on the fork and pressed down heavily, displacing the soil around the rose bush she was currently working on. She pulled the handle of the fork horizontally to the soil, ensuring its prongs moved the dirt upward. She continued to do this until the earth around the bush was completely dug up and turned over.

Her mother's rose garden needed to be prepared for the incoming frost. Autumn was coming to a fast close, with the tree's leaves having almost all fallen to the ground and the winter chill coming in from further up north. Before they knew it would be winter. The temperature so far was already in the low twenties.

For the roses and the other flowers in the garden to have another successful blooming session next spring, what she was doing now was very important to prevent the frost from destroying them. She made a note that she needed to pick up some bags of mulch and garden coverings from the garden store when next she visited town.

She rested against the fork and wiped the sweat from her brows.

Resting a bit, she admired the beauty before her. A plethora of colorful roses and other flowers, those that were perennial and those that were annual, perpetuated the space broken up and separated by cobbled pathways that gave visitors the opportunity to admire the work of art that was her mother's rose garden.

A small smile of satisfaction graced her lips. It was a lot of work to prepare the garden for the winter, but she was prepared for it.

"Need a hand?"

Andrea looked over her shoulders to see her sisters coming toward her.

"Thanks, but I think this is it for me today," she informed them, taking in a deep breath and releasing it before turning to join them on the path.

"You know Jamie did offer to send a few of his workers to help out. It's not too late to accept the offer," Cora suggested as they made their way toward the raised platform to the back of the garden.

"I know, but I just think this is something we should take care of ourselves. Dad took great pride in making this garden beautiful for mom all by himself. We owe it to him and to ourselves to continue his work knowing all that we know."

The three sisters sank into the garden chairs situated around a wrought iron table. Cora released a heavy sigh.

"I'm so scared at how quickly mom's sickness is progressing," she spoke fearfully.

The others nodded their agreement, the weight of what was now proving to be the inevitable pressing heavily on them. They were witnessing all that the doctor had explained to them would happen, and from their own research that their mother was manifesting more and more of the symptoms posted for stage two. Pretty soon, she would progress to stage three. None of them could bear the thought.

"I keep wondering...if we had known earlier. If we had come back sooner, if it would have made a difference, you know?" Andrea peered at her sisters, her face riddled with guilt and regret. These were the questions that plagued her constantly, especially at night when she lay in bed.

"You can't think like that," Cora warned. "It's not our fault that mom is sick, and as much as I do wish we had known earlier, I'm not sure it would have made much difference. You heard what the doctor said. Even if she could be admitted to a trial, there was only a 25% chance that it would have prolonged her life for a few more years."

The sisters sat in silence for a while, each lost in their own thought and regrets over the whole situation. It didn't seem fair to Andrea. She was just rebuilding her relationship with her mother and running out of time fast.

"It kills me to see her in so much pain," Jo sighed, looking down at her locked fingers resting on the table.

"Yeah, I know," Cora agreed. "I wish she wouldn't try to hide just how much pain she's really in. This morning I heard her groaning, but when I went into her room, she stopped and tried covering it with a smile, but I could see it in her eyes. She was struggling." Cora shuddered, dismayed by the memory.

"The day you guys went dress shopping with Rory, she had another episode," Jo confessed softly.

"What?" Andrea and Cora gasped simultaneously.

Jo lifted her head to look at her sisters, her expression pained. "We were in the living room watching a game show, and she started laughing. I thought it was because the host had given a joke and she enjoyed it but then she wouldn't stop, and she started crying immediately afterward, just like she'd done our last Sunday get-together. When I went to check on her, her hand was curled in on itself, and I couldn't pry it open. It was so stiff," she whispered the last sentence. "When I tried to get her to stand up to take her to her room, she couldn't move." Jo looked at her sisters, tears pooling at the corners of her eyes. "It was like she was paralyzed from the waist down. I panicked at first, but then I gave her the medication the doctors prescribed. It took more than an hour to get her up the stairs after that."

Andrea sighed, saddened by her sister's revelation. "We need to get her to the ground floor," she expressed. "Also, I think it's time we considered buying one of the full electric hospital beds and possibly consider getting her a motorized scooter."

The others nodded their agreement.

Another pause ensued.

"I know we have to accept what is going to happen soon, but it doesn't make it any easier especially knowing that she has to suffer in so much pain during the process."

"I'm just glad that Rory will be having her wedding here so mom can get to attend. I think that will do so much for her."

"Yeah. I'm glad too," Cora responded.

"This is what we need these moments for new memories. It can't make up for the ones we lost, but at least mom will get to feel how much we love her."

"What's wrong?" Cora asked, noticing that Andrea wore a far-off look.

She turned to look at the sister. "I don't know…It feels like there is something going on with Rory that she's not telling me about, and I'm worried. She doesn't seem herself. I've been worried since she told me that she wanted to take a break from work."

"What do you think it might be?" Josephine asked.

"Whatever it is, I think it has a lot to do with James," she revealed her suspicions.

The sisters turned to look at her attentively, waiting for further explanation.

"About a week ago, I heard her on the phone with James. She was telling him that either they have the wedding here in Oak Harbor or they don't have it all. When I questioned her about it, she said his mother wanted them to have the wedding in San Francisco— that she insisted that they should get married in San Fran. I told her that it was a decision for her and James to make. She was worried that they weren't on the same page, though." Andrea sighed. "It just feels like there is a whole lot more to this story than she's letting on."

Her sisters reached out to give her arm a reassuring squeeze.

"I think I should find out from James what's wrong."

"Drea..." Cora spoke with caution. "I don't think that's wise."

"But what else is there to do? I'm not going to get the answers from her," she reasoned.

"I know how you feel, Drea. The helplessness of it all. I remember I wanted to reach Julia to find out why and how she got pregnant. I wanted to go to Washington State and speak to her friends to find out what happened, but I had to clamp down on my desire to get to the bottom of it all and just trust that she'll tell me when she's ready. Dealing with Jules is like handling fragile glassware. The tiniest mistake leads to breaks and lost trust." Cora released a long breath. "I keep wondering if I could have prevented what happened instead of being judgmental and trying to get her to march to my tune instead of her own. I should have listened more." Cora sighed defeatedly.

"She still hasn't told you who the father is?" Andrea asked.

"No," Cora replied. "She changes the subject every time I ask."

Andrea gave her sister a sympathetic look.

"Tracy and I are enjoying a more open relationship," Jo chimed in. "Since everything her father had been doing came to light and I explained why I hid it from her, we have been doing much better."

"That's good news. I'm happy for you, Jo," Andrea congratulated. "I wish it had worked for Rory and me. It's like even though I know she has forgiven me for lying about her father that there is still a slight wedge between us. There has never been a time that she's kept anything from me."

"Don't give up. Just continue showing her that you're there for her," Jo encouraged.

Andrea nodded.

The sisters left to go back to the house. Andrea sat thinking over all they'd shared with her. She knew they were probably right that she shouldn't try to call her son-in-law to find out what was happening, but she needed answers. It felt like if she waited too long to get the answers, it would be too late.

Reaching into her pants pocket, she took out her phone and dialed James. He answered on the second ring.

"Hello?"

"How is my favorite son-in-law doing?" she cajoled, a bright smile on her lips to match.

"Hi, Mom," James greeted. "I'm happy to hear your voice."

She noted that he skirted away from answering her original question.

"Are you all right?" she asked directly.

There was a pause before he responded. "I'm fine, Mom... I'm just tired. I've had a very busy couple of weeks, and I'm still busy," he explained.

"Don't work yourself to the bone, James. You have to save some of your energy for your wedding day and wedding night."

James laughed at this. "I'll try not to overexert myself," he promised.

"Good," Andrea grinned happily before sobering up. "I'm actually calling because I need to ask you something."

"Sounds serious." There was an edge to his tone, she noted.

"Yes. Rory. I think there is something wrong with her, but I don't know what it is. I was hoping you might know."

At the palpable silence, she pushed.

"James, is there something going on between you and Rory that you're both not telling me?"

Chapter Thirteen

Rory burrowed further under the thick comforter, protecting herself from the cold permeating the room and threatening to leave hair-raising goosebumps prickling her skin. She could tell that the thermostat needed adjustment but was too tired to go downstairs. Plus, the warmth from the comforter securely cushioning her made it less expedient to do so. All she wanted to do was enjoy the last hour or so of unbothered sleep before she had to face the new day. Her brows drew into a frown at the sudden vibration jerking the bed, making it difficult for her to slip deeper into a world of dreams. Trying to get away from the disturbance, she turned to lay on her side.

The annoying staccato humming was in her head, making her temple pulse like a beaten drum as her eyes rolled under tightly closed lids. She rolled onto her stomach slid out her hand across the bed, searching. A few seconds later, her fingers came in contact with the object of her discomfort, and she wrapped them around it. Without opening her eyes, she brought it to her ear.

"Hello?" she answered, her voice still groggy with sleep.

"Hi."

"James?" Rory's eyes blinked open.

"Yes, it's me," he confirmed with a light chuckle. "I saw your call...I'm sorry I missed it. I had a lot on my plate yesterday," he explained. "I should have seen it and called back right away. I'm sorry."

"No, it's fine," Rory assured him, drawing herself up until her back met the headboard. "I was calling because...I just wanted to hear your voice," she spoke softly.

Rory cast her eyes downward to stare at the floral patterns of the comforter now lying across the lower half of her body as she waited for her fiancé to respond.

"I miss you."

Rory drew in a deep breath at his confession as her heartbeat wildly against her chest. "I miss you too," she answered, her free hand creeping up to rest against her heart.

James sighed. "I wish I could be there with you right now, but Gary doubled my workload. He says the more cases I work on and the more clients I have on retainer, the better my chances of making partner next year. But these cases..." He sighed again. "The case on Jared Finch is a real headache."

"Wanna talk about it?" Rory asked.

"I can't..."

"Oh, yeah...right...I forgot. So, I found a dress."

"You did? That's wow, that's great."

"Yeah. Mom and I went dress shopping in Seattle. The moment I saw it, I knew it was the one." A smile broke out on her face as she thought back to how right it felt the minute she saw her reflection in the mirror. She knew that dress was the one that she wanted to walk down the aisle in— to marry James.

"I can't wait to see you in it."

Her smile brightened. "I also booked a florist. She's local. My cousin Kerry recommended her."

"Okay, that's good too," James replied, committed to the conversation.

"We need to decide on the menu. The caterer sent some samples for us to choose from. I have an idea of what I want, but I needed your input too."

"Okay. What are they?" he asked.

Rory rattled off the items from each menu idea from the top of her head.

"I think either menus one or three could work for our guests," James supplied. "But, as long as I get to call you my wife at the end of this, it doesn't matter to me what is served— it could be Kraft Dinner for all I care. I just want to marry you."

Rory's heart skipped a beat at his declaration, and her grip around the phone tightened. "I'm planning to stay in Oak Harbor for Thanksgiving," she informed him, her voice low and hesitant.

"Oh...I thought...okay."

Her stomach knotted at the obvious disappointment in his tone. "What are your plans for the weekend?" She brought her knees up to her chest to rest her chin on top of them.

"I'm attending a function with Mom and Dad...a gala," he informed her. "It's a fundraiser for advancements in cancer research. If you ask me, it's just an excuse for all the rich folks to get together and flaunt their wealth, but mom already paid for my seat, so I have no choice but to attend."

Her face fell. After his revelation that he missed her, she thought he would have at least tried to come and see her or even would have begged her to come home. Instead, as busy as he claimed to be, he had time to attend events with his parents. Even if they paid for his seat, she thought he could have still declined the invite. It felt like he had time for everyone and everything else but her. A chill coursed through her that had nothing to do with the coldness of her room.

"Are you still there?" James asked after a minute of silence.

"I am," she breathed out.

"Are you all right?"

"Mmhmm," she responded, the pitch of her voice sharply rising at the end.

"Are you sure?" he pressed.

"I am," she reaffirmed. "Have a good time at the gala," she continued to say, moving the conversation away from her.

"Thanks...I'll try," he spoke with uncertainty.

Rory felt wetness on her face. Reaching up to touch the spot, she realized that silent tears had been flowing. *Why couldn't James realize that she was miserable? Why couldn't he pick up that she wanted him to come for her?* Gripping the edge of the comforter, she tugged it upward and bent her head to allow the fabric to run across her cheeks, wiping at the evidence of her melancholy. *Why couldn't he fight for her like she was expecting him to?*

"Is your mom okay? She called two days ago..."

"Mom called you?" Rory's brows raised in surprise. "What did she say?"

"She asked me if something was wrong between us," he revealed.

"What?" she nearly screeched.

"Yeah. She said she was worried about us. Did you say anything to her?"

"I didn't." Rory sighed, lowering her head to her lap again.

"Your mom isn't a fool, Rory."

She moved her head back and forth where it lay, agreeing with his statement even though he couldn't see her. It was a fact; Andrea wasn't easily fooled. She was very smart and observant. Rory just couldn't believe that she went behind her back to call James to ask about their relationship.

"I know she isn't," came her muffled reply. Raising her head to look across the room, she continued. "I just didn't expect her to do this."

"She's worried about you, Rory... about us."

Her eyes fluttered shut in thought.

"Listen, I gotta go. I need to get to the office to get some documents before heading to meet a client."

Rory looked over at the glowing green numbers on the clock that sat atop the bedside table. It read 4:55 AM.

"I'll call you when I get in later."

"Okay," she responded slowly. "Talk to you later."

"Rory?"

"Yeah?"

"I love you."

Her heart ceased to beat for a millisecond before assuming its regular pattern. "Bye, James."

After disconnecting the call, she leaned back against the headboard with her eyes closed. She still couldn't believe Andrea had gone behind her back. Unable to close her eyes, she flung the comforter off her feet and went to her closet. She removed a pair of sweatpants and a hoodie. When she finished dressing in them, she put her hair up in a high bun and slipped on her sneakers. Making her way to the foyer, she went over to the thermostat and adjusted the temperature before heading for the door.

The moment she stepped out onto the porch, the cold autumn air blasted her, the icy chill already stinging her cheeks. She was sure they were the color of fresh, ripe tomatoes. Reaching for one end of the plaid woolen scarf around her neck, she wound it around the lower half of her face.

Descending the three wide front steps, she began a quick trot and transitioned into a jog down the path. The sky was a mixture of magenta, orange, and blue painted clouds, heralding the arrival of dawn.

A Spectacular Event

Rory loved the feel of her feet hitting the cobbled stone path as she ran between the flowers and shrubs forming barriers on either side. The sound of her own breath elevating and collapsing her chest was the only sound keeping her company. Five minutes into her run, she passed the restaurant. The neon welcome sign flashed in the window.

A smile widened Rory's lips when she noticed Chef Daniel and her aunt Jo with their arms thrown around each other as they lightly swayed in the open space between a few tables to what she could only assume was music they were playing. She guessed she wasn't the only one that had an early start to the day. A couple of minutes later, she was running past the inn. She could see the light streaming out from a few of the guest rooms. When she made it to the turn that led off the property, she decided to retrace her steps back to the main house, but instead of heading inside, she made her way down to the harbor. As she looked out across the horizon, the orange streaks in the sky brightened to a light golden hue as the sun began to make its appearance. Her conversation with James flashed through her thoughts and left her feeling colder than the wind running across her exposed skin. With a long, heavy sigh, she turned toward the house.

The aroma of cinnamon hit her nostrils when she opened the back door, assuaging her senses and causing her mouth to salivate. Walking through the kitchen door, she found her mother by the island, cutting out cookie dough.

"Hi, sweetie," Andrea looked up to greet her before turning her attention back to the dough.

"Hey," she returned, non-committal.

"How was your run?"

"Fine." Rory swiped an apple from the fruit bowl and sauntered toward the sink. Turning on the tap, she allowed the cold water to run over the fruit, cleaning it. She turned around, her eyes connected with her mother, who stood staring intently at her. She raised a brow in question.

"Is everything okay?" Andrea asked, her voice filled with concern.

"Yeah. it is." Rory answered in a clipped tone.

"Are you sure?" her mother carefully asked.

"Yes, mother. Everything is fine," she repeated with finality. With that, she walked toward the kitchen exit before stopping in the entrance way abruptly. Andrea walked to the other side of the island, watching her daughter with perplexity.

"You know what, Mom?" she asked, turning around to face her mother. "Everything is not fine," she blew up, throwing her hands in the air.

Andrea's brows rose in a slow arch of confusion.

"How could you call James behind my back like that?"

Andrea's eyes widened. Recovering from her stupor, she took a step toward her daughter. "Rory I—"

"I told you that everything was fine. James and I are fine, but still, you had to call him. That is not cool, Mom! My word should be enough for you to stay out of my personal life. I won't let you control this narrative like you did with my father." By this time, angry tears were rolling down her cheeks.

"Rory, that wasn't what I was trying to do," Andrea tried to explain. "It's just that you looked so miserable, and what you told me about James' mother, I just felt like there was something going on...something that you're not telling me, and I just wanted to help."

Rory fixed her mother an angry stare. "When I need your help, I will ask for it. In the meantime, stay out of my personal life." Rory stormed out of the kitchen, but instead of heading upstairs, she headed for the back porch and made her way back to the harbor.

As she stared out at the blue-green waters reflecting the

risen golden sun, she recalled how she spoke to her mom. She released her tight grip around her chest, allowing her arms to fall to her sides, her shoulders sagging as guilt set in and her tears flowed.

Chapter Fourteen

Rory wasn't sure where she wanted to go. She just knew that she had to get out of the house and away from her mother. After their big blowout, a myriad of emotions coursed through her. On one end, she was ashamed of the way she spoke to her mother, but on the other hand, she was angry with her for interfering in her life. She just needed to go somewhere that she could blow off some steam. As she drove downtown, it was evident that finding a quiet spot would be difficult. It seemed everyone was out and about, probably making early Christmas purchases to avoid the rush coming next month. She was planning to do her own shopping during the Black Friday and Cyber Monday blowout sales herself.

As she passed the marina, something told her to pull over. Without hesitation, she pulled up to the curb before walking up to the boardwalk.

She leaned over the railing to look out at the pristine water glistening under the bright rays. There were a few fishing boats out on the horizon with a troupe of birds trailing them.

She sighed heavily. Her life felt like a mess, but it had nothing to do with her mother. She should have expected Andrea to try to get to the bottom of what was going on with her. Before everyone and everything else, it had always been just the two of them, and she knew her mother would do anything to make sure she was okay. She remembered that well about her— even if it meant going without or sacrificing her own well-being, she would. That was just the type of mother she had. It still didn't give her the right to go behind her back. She knew she had to apologize for the way she reacted eventually but right now, she just wanted to hold on to the anger she felt, especially as she wasn't able to tell her mother-in-law how she truly felt about her and her meddling ways. She knew Lenora was still scheming to sabotage her wedding and that she had something to do with James not having any free time to himself, but she didn't have proof. But she was also angry at James, angry that he couldn't tell how much she needed to see him. Their wedding was a little over a month away, and yet it felt like she was alone in all of this. For what seemed like the umpteenth time, she wasn't sure if this wedding would actually take place come December 23rd, nor if she wanted to walk down that aisle.

She felt more lost and frustrated than she'd been when she had just gotten there. With another heavy sigh, she started to head back to her car when she noticed a young man walking in her direction with his head down, his hands in the pockets of the green hoodie sweater he wore over a pair of skinny black jeans and white sneakers. What caught her attention was his cropped dirty blond hair and the angular features of his face, so similar to his father's.

"Trey?"

The young man's head snapped up, his blue eyes registering surprise.

"Hi," he greeted hesitantly.

"Hi. What are you doing out here? Shouldn't you be on campus now?"

Trey shrugged his shoulders. "I only had an exam today. That's over with, so…"

Rory nodded her understanding.

"What are you doing out here?" he returned.

She gave him a tight-lipped smile before answering. "I had some free time, too," she replied vaguely.

"Are you leaving now?" he asked, looking behind him before turning his gaze back to her.

"I was…what're you…are you here with someone?" Rory averted her eyes, trying to see who was behind him, but her gaze came up empty.

"No, I'm not," he confirmed. The two stood in awkward silence for a few seconds before Trey spoke up. "I'm gonna get a hot dog by the stand over there. Want one?"

Rory hesitated. She opened her mouth to decline the offer but at the last minute said, "Sure. Why not?" Maybe this was the perfect opportunity for her to get to know the young man better, plus she was hungry. She'd skipped breakfast, and the only thing she'd eaten all day was the apple from the kitchen. It was almost midday now. Her stomach grumbled as if on cue just then.

She gave Trey a sheepish look. "Sorry about that. I haven't eaten all day."

"Don't sweat it," the young man responded, his lips broadening into a reassuring smile.

With that, she followed him toward the hotdog stand, just a few feet away from the boardwalk.

After the two collected their order, they strolled down the boardwalk before settling on one of the double benches along the side. They immediately dug into their hotdogs, foregoing making small talk as they filled their stomachs.

In between bites, Rory took the time to continue admiring

the small boats and yachts moored by the docks swaying back and forth, ready to be boarded and driven out to the open waters. The cloudless sky was the bluest she'd ever remembered seeing it.

She took a swig from the bottle of water she bought and turned to scrutinize Trey's side profile.

"What?" he asked after more than ten seconds of her unwavering gaze. He turned to face her; his brows scrunched together in confusion.

"Nothing," she replied simply, returning to her meal.

"It must be something. You were staring like you were waiting for me to combust in flames or something," Trey summarized.

Rory lowered the hotdog and turned to look at him with a small unsure smile.

"I was just wondering if everything is okay with you."

"Yeah. Why wouldn't it?" he asked, making a face as he looked at her like the question was stupid.

"Okay. I'm sorry I asked. You're obviously fine." She turned back to look out across the open ocean.

"I want to be a firefighter."

Rory craned her necked to the side to look up at Trey, waiting for him to continue.

"I want to be a firefighter, but my dad wants me to get a college degree." His shoulders rose and fell as he sagged against the bench.

Her head slowly bobbed in thought. "How old are you?"

"I'm nineteen. Old enough to join the department, old enough to become an officer or even a soldier," he listed, the frustration in his voice telling.

"I totally get that. I wasn't implying that you couldn't. I'm just trying to understand your father's reasoning," she explained.

"He thinks that if I go to college, it'll give me a fairer shot in life, but..." He brought his palms up and ran them down his face before resting his elbows on his thighs and leaning forward. He clasped his hands under his chin, his fingers intertwining to support its weight. After a few more seconds of him not saying anything, he finally released his hands and straightened up.

"I've wanted to be a firefighter since I was a little boy. But more than anything, I've always wanted to be like my dad. He loves his job and the people that he gets to call his work family and the respect that they have for him, not to mention the community...I remember when I was a kid, maybe five or six, the first time I saw my dad on the news, I was just so blown away by the gears he was wearing, the soot on his face and just how he spoke with confidence and assurance after he and his team rescued a whole apartment building of people." Trey paused to look over at Rory, a smile on his lips, his eyes twinkling in reminiscence. "The reporter asked him how it felt to be a hero in his own right...his reply was that he didn't see himself as a hero but rather one who has the privilege of serving his community and saving lives in the process. Then the reporter said that the world needed more men who were willing to serve as well as he did, and, at that moment, I knew I wanted to be a firefighter."

Rory smiled back at him with understanding and admiration. "I can tell that you're going to make a great firefighter," she complimented.

A noticeable red hue ran up the sides of his neck. Trey ducked his head even as his smile broadened.

"I'm going to say something, and I don't want you to take it the wrong way," Rory continued to say, still staring at the young man to gauge his reaction.

Trey's blue eyes cut to her.

After drawing in a small breath and releasing it, she explained, "I think your father is fine with you becoming a firefighter, but he might feel that just being that is limiting your ability to function outside of that space. Being a firefighter is a dangerous job Trey, and that makes it very unpredictable. I think Donny wants you to do the degree so that in case anything happens, you'll still have a fair shot at life. Look at it this way. Being a firefighter has been your dream, your passion for all these years you've not wavered. What's a couple more years of waiting and a college degree?"

Trey nodded his head in understanding.

"Your father will have no choice but to see you as a smart and responsible young man and respect your choices."

He continued to nod as he cast his eyes down in thought. Finally, he looked over at her, his blue eyes warm with mirth. "You know, you're kinda cool. If I had a big sister, I'd like to imagine that she would have been just like you— smart, take no nonsense, sensitive, caring, and I think I already said smart."

Rory felt the heat creep up her neck before it settled in her cheeks. Her lips broadened involuntarily. It was her turn to duck her head. She leaned into him, bumping their shoulders. "You're not so bad yourself. I suppose if I had a little brother, I would imagine him being just like you too— stubborn, rude—"

"Hey!" Trey called out in offense.

Rory held up her hand as laughter bubbled in her chest. "Let me finish," she implored. "He'd be passionate, and he'd have a big heart that he tries to hide on occasions but can't." She smiled brightly at him, letting him see how sincere she was.

Trey happily returned her smile.

If she had a brother, she definitely would have wanted him to be like him. It was humbling how far their relationship had come since their first meeting. On the two occasions that they got to be alone, he'd shown her his vulnerable side, and she'd come to understand him more, and now she really did appreciate their budding brother-sister relationship, especially with him trying to get along with her mother. But just then her mood soured at the thought of her mother.

"What about you?"

Rory looked over at him from the corner of her eye, her head tilting with the action in his direction.

"What about me?" she asked skeptically.

Trey turned fully to stare at her side profile. "Why did you come to the boardwalk Rory?" he asked, all the humor gone from his tone.

This time she turned, looking over at him. His eyes seemed much older and wiser than his years as they peered at her.

She sighed. He'd confided so much about his own struggles to her that she owed him the courtesy of some explanation.

She drew in a deep gulp of air, expanding her lungs to twice their capacity before releasing it. "I got in an argument with my mom earlier this morning," she revealed.

He nodded in encouragement for her to explain.

"My fiancé, James and I are having some problems, and it has really been stressing me out. Mom went behind my back and called him..." She went on to offer more details and vent her frustrations. Trey nodded his understanding of all that she'd said.

When she finally finished expressing herself, it felt like a boulder had been lifted off her shoulders.

"From what I can tell, your mom loves you very much," Trey offered after a minute of complete silence. "She's worried that something's wrong, and she took it in her mind to mean that you are in trouble and have been trying to solve this for you. I'll give you the same advice you gave me. Don't be so hard on her."

At that, Rory smiled, knowing her was right. Even though she wanted her mother to stay out of her personal issues, she knew Andrea was only trying to help.

Chapter Fifteen

"Hi, sweetie. Can we talk?"

Rory looked up from stirring her coffee to see her mother standing in the entryway, cautiously staring at her.

"Hi, Mom. Yeah, sure. I have something that I need to say to you as well."

Her mother's steps were hesitant, but she finally made it to the kitchen island and took a seat across from her. Andrea looked at the steaming beverage before she looked up at Rory, her eyes filled with concern. "Did you eat?"

Rory looked into the dark liquid, the steam meandering its way upward to permeate her nostrils and the rest of the kitchen with its rich, aromatic scent. Her gaze rose to her mother. "I ate a hot dog earlier today," she revealed.

Her mother's eyes widened in alarm.

"And that's the only thing you ate?"

Rory nodded. "Oh, I ate an apple before that," she added, snapping her fingers.

"But that was hours ago. It's after midnight now. I put your dinner in the refrigerator. Let me pop it in the microwave for you."

Andrea went to get up, but Rory quickly stopped her with a raise of her palm. "It's fine. Seriously. I'm not really that hungry."

"Are you sure?" her mother questioned. "At least let me get you a slice of the apple pie. I made it today," she pressed.

Rory was about to decline, but..." That would be great. Thanks, Mom."

Andrea smiled in relief as she made her way over to the refrigerator to remove the pie. Rory watched her mother plate a sizeable piece of pie. It triggered a broad smile on her lips. *How could she stay angry at her?* She'd always been the one who helped her face her fears and stood up for her over and over again. She knew Andrea would give up her own happiness if it meant her happiness. It dawned on her that, that was what she'd done all those years. She had been carrying around the guilt of Rory's father not wanting her and had done everyone in her power to make his absence not affect her in the way it could have, had she known he was alive and didn't want her. Her mother had truly sacrificed a considerable deal to protect her.

"Mom, I'm sorry about this morning."

Her mother, who had been walking in her direction with the pie, faltered in her tracks, and her eyes widened in surprise as her lips formed in an 'o'.

Rory took the opportunity to continue. "I was angry, and I said some unkind things to you. I want you to know that I appreciate you and everything you've done for me and continue to do."

"Oh, sweetie," Andrea exhaled, resting the pie before her. "I'm sorry that I went behind your back like that. You have every right to be angry with me."

Rory shook her head in refusal. Her mother placed her hand on her cheek, stilling her movement.

A Spectacular Event

"I betrayed your trust, and I shouldn't have done that. I need you to understand that and.... I also want you to know that I'm worried about you, but I'll wait until you're ready to tell me what's going on because that's what it means to trust."

Rory reached up to squeeze the hand on her cheek as she stared at her mother gratefully.

"I love you, mom," she stated, her green eyes shining bright with affection.

Andrea brought her arms around her daughter and hugged her close to her chest. Rory mirrored her mother's actions, standing from the stool to bring them closer. "I love you too, my sweet, sweet girl. I just want you to be happy," Andrea breathed against her temple.

"Mom... there's something I need to tell you," Rory spoke solemnly. Dropping her arms, she stepped away from her mother. She retook her seat at the island. Andrea sat on the stool beside her and stood to face her. Rory gulped and turned her eyes to her mother.

"James' parents don't like me, and they're against the wedding. They wanted him to marry someone they chose for him...someone from their own social group."

"What?" Andrea almost screeched. She closed her eyes and drew in a deep breath. "What does James have to say about it?" she asked calmly.

Rory's eyes fluttered downward. "He keeps telling me that it doesn't matter what they think, he's marrying me regardless, and that should be enough." Her eyes connected with her mother's, moisture pooling in them. "I don't think that's enough for me, Mom," she revealed, her voice gutted. "He doesn't understand just how much this is affecting me. I came here because I needed some space to think, but..." Rory turned to look at her mother, eyes now glistening with her unshed tears. "I thought he would miss me enough to come to get me or at least beg me to come home, but it seems like he's been doing okay without me."

"Oh, Rory. I'm so sorry this is happening to you," Andrea relayed sympathetically, pulling her daughter toward her chest.

A tear ran down Rory's cheek as her mother lovingly smoothed her hand over her hair. "I miss him, Mom." A sob escaped her lips.

"I know, sweetie," Andrea soothed. After a few minutes of allowing Rory to release her pent-up emotions, she spoke. "I know it might not look like it now, honey, but I know that man loves you more than anything and that he misses you dearly." She lifted Rory's head, palming her cheeks as she stared at her seriously. "Forget what his mother and father think. Whatever they've been trying hasn't worked, and I'm guessing they've been trying hard to sabotage this wedding...am I right?"

Rory slowly nodded before averting her eyes. If her mother only knew how hard they'd been trying, especially Lenora, she was sure she would be on the next flight to San Fran to confront them. She didn't want that, especially with the nuptials being so close. For that reason, she opted to keep the information about the prenup to herself.

"Don't worry about them. They don't matter, and nothing they do ever will. I'll make sure of it." A mutinous expression crossed her face, her blue eyes steely with determination. Rory's heart slammed against her chest with anxiety.

"Mom...please don't."

Andrea looked down at her daughter. "What? I wasn't planning on confronting them...at least not in the way you're thinking," she smiled slightly. That didn't fill Rory with assurance. She gave her mother a look of skepticism.

"I promise, I won't do anything out of the ordinary...as long as it is not warranted."

"Mom..."

Andrea pressed her lips against her daughter's temple before moving her head back to look at her again. "I love you, sweetheart. There is nothing I wouldn't do for you. I want you to know that."

That was what Rory was afraid of.

"Just promise me you won't say anything to them when they get here. Better yet, it would be great if you could sit at the opposite end for the reception," she implored.

"That wouldn't be very family-like, now would it, sweetheart? Besides, I think it would be a great idea to show the Davises just how loving of a family we are."

Rory sighed, fearing that would only make the problem worse.

"Sweetie," Andrea said, bringing her daughter's attention back to her. "They. Don't. Matter," she reiterated. "What matters is that you are marrying the man of your dreams. The man who knows you're good enough for him, just the way you are."

"Thanks, Mom. I needed that."

Andrea placed another kiss against her temple. "No need to thank me, I'm your mother, and that's what mothers do."

"Still, I want you to know just how much I appreciate you and everything that you've ever done for me." Rory reached over and placed a loving kiss against her mother's cheek. "You are one in a million."

Andrea smiled warmly at her.

Rory finally turned her attention to the forgotten pie and reached for the fork. "Let me get in a few bites of this before it gets cold again."

"I have an idea."

Rory raised a curious brow at her mother.

"Some Ben & Jerry's would go really great with this, and we could stay up a little longer and maybe watch some 'I Love Lucy," she suggested.

"Do we have double fudge brownie?" Rory asked.

"Let me check." Andrea opened the freezer before reaching her hand inside. She turned around with a tub of ice cream in her hand and a broad smile on her lips. "We're in luck," she spoke triumphantly.

"Yay!" Rory exclaimed, doing a little jiggle.

"Looks like we're just in time to join the party."

She looked to the kitchen's entrance to see both her aunts there with semi-perplexed grins on their faces.

"Hi, guys. We were gonna veg out in front of the TV in the family room," Andrea explained.

"Cool. We'll join you. We haven't done that in a while."

Soon the four women with their own spoons and two tubs of ice cream headed for the den. Andrea turned on the DVD player and popped in the disk before settling among the cushions they'd strew out on the carpet with the others.

As the first episode of 'I love Lucy' came on, so did a smile of contentment on Rory's face as she viewed the women who all formed an integral part of her life in some way or the other. She had to admit, she loved their commitment and the love that they showed her. She only wished they'd had this opportunity much earlier. She'd visited her aunts a bunch of times back in their old lives, but it never felt like this. Here is Oak Harbor, she'd felt more connected to them like they were a true family.

"I know this won't end well."

Rory looked over at her aunt Jo, who'd just spoken as they watched the title character and her friend working at a chocolate factory hiding chocolate in their hats and blouses and even packing their mouths because they couldn't wrap them fast enough to prevent them from reaching the packing room unwrapped.

"It wouldn't be an 'I love Lucy' episode if something didn't go unnaturally wrong," Cora agreed with a snort.

They all burst into laughter when the conveyer doubled,

and the character's antics became even more hilarious. Rory doubled over, holding her tummy as she heaved. She'd seen this episode before, but she had to admit that the more she saw it, the funnier it got.

"Lucille Ball is a national treasure," Andrea declared between laughs.

"Yup. There will never be another actress so naturally funny," Jo agreed.

The women settled down to continue watching the episode, chuckling at intervals, and scooping spoonful's of ice cream into their mouths.

"I think it's time to call it a night," Cora said, rising to her feet and stretching.

"Or day," Jo replied, jutting her chin toward the grandfather clock in the corner reading 2:30 am. "Are you guys going back to bed?" she directed at Andrea and Rory.

"In a minute," Andrea responded.

"All right, see you guys in the morning...I mean later in the day."

"Goodnight," Rory and Andrea said in unison.

Rory turned to her mother with a wide grin. "I really enjoyed this," she revealed.

"Me too, sweetie," Andrea responded. "You know, everything will work out," she continued to say, squeezing her daughter's arm warmly. "No matter what, I'll always be here for you."

"I know," Rory agreed.

"All right, it's time for this old woman to get some shut-eye."

"Hey, you're not old. You're too cool for that," Rory defended.

Andrea laughed, the sound filling her daughter's chest with warmth.

After repositioning the cushions in the chairs, the two ascended the stairs to get to their rooms.

Rory crossed the room to sit on her bed. She reached for the phone on the bedside table and flipped through her missed calls and messages. Her smile slowly fell when she realized James hadn't called as he had promised.

Chapter Sixteen

Andrea's eyes slowly fluttered open, but they felt like some weight was on them, forcing them back down, but as soon as they shut, the blaring sound of her alarm forced them back up, reminding her why she'd chosen to wake up in the first place. She rolled over unto her belly and stretched her arm across to reach the source of her annoyance. She tapped the device until it ceased to make a sound.

After a few minutes of contemplating whether or not she should get up or snuggle down in her warm, cozy bed, she released an exaggerated sigh before propping herself up on her elbows until she was sitting in the middle of the bed. Today was her day to make mom's breakfast before heading to the inn to help out. After another release of breath, she scooted to the edge of the bed and swung her legs over and stood up and headed for the bathroom.

Andrea sighed with relief as the warm water splashed over her cold, achy muscles. "Thank God for hot water," she thought. Ten minutes later, she was drawing on a pair of blue jeans and a white T-shirt with the Statue of Liberty in the front and the Empire State building on the back.

Just as she slipped on her sandals, her cell phone rang. She reached down to pick it up. A giddy smile swept across her face at the name displayed.

"Hey, you," she greeted, sitting down on the bed.

"Hi. How'd you sleep?"

"I didn't get much sleep," she revealed.

"Why not? Are you okay? Do you want me to get anything for you?"

"I'm fine," she giggled. A hand reached up to cover her lips, mortified by how childish it sounded. "I'm sorry about that," she apologized.

"Why? I like it. It's cute. You can giggle anytime for me."

Andrea felt her cheeks flush as the butterflies in her stomach did summersaults. "Anyway, I didn't get much sleep because I stayed up talking with Rory. We had a blowout yesterday, but we're good now."

"I'm sorry to hear that, but I'm glad you're both okay now... Trey mentioned that he saw her down at the boardwalk."

"Oh really? So that's where she went," Andrea replied more to herself than Donny.

"Don't quote me on it, but I think he really likes your daughter. I've never heard him talk about anyone with such admiration the way he talks about Rory."

"Wow, that's...that's...I mean. It's going far better than I initially expected," Andrea confessed, feeling in awe.

"The kids are all right," Donny chuckled.

"Are you quoting from that 70s show?" Andrea quirked her brow even though he couldn't see her.

"I am," he confirmed.

Andrea released a soft chuckle.

"I can't wait to see you later."

Andrea shivered slightly at the deep drop in his voice.

"I can't wait to see you too," she all but whispered shyly as a coy smile turned her lips slightly upward.

After a few more minutes of them ironing out the details for their date, Andrea hung up from Donny and headed downstairs to prep Becky's meal.

As she neared the kitchen, she could hear slight whimpers. Alarmed, she hastened her steps. She found Julia with her head resting on her arms that were being supported by the island.

Andrea cautiously approached her niece, whom it was evident was in pain. "Jules...are you okay?" she asked, resting her arms on the young woman's back.

Julia turned her head upward to look at Andrea, who was now staring down at her in concern. A wave of protectiveness came over Andrea at the grimace of pain on her face.

"Sweetie, what's wrong?" she cajoled.

"I-I'm f-f-fi...ne," Julia forced out.

"You don't seem fine," Andrea refuted.

"It's just Braxton-Hick's contractions...they'll pass soon," Julia tried to convince her even while her eyes and lips tightened as she released a low moan of discomfort."

"Do you want me to get your mom?"

"N-No," she responded forcefully.

Andrea opened her mouth, ready to argue that it was the best option, but Julia beat her to it.

"Aunty Drea, I don't want to worry mom with something that's as natural as breathing. I'm fine, I promise. The doctor said when I feel contractions, I should check for spotting, and if there's none, then it probably means everything is fine. I checked. Everything is fine."

Andrea opened and closed her mouth like a fish out of water. All the arguments she'd prepared had been made moot by her niece's summations. "Okay...I'll let it go. For now, if the contractions start to get too unbearable or too frequent, tell your mother. Better yet, call your obstetrician."

"Thanks, Auntie," Julia smiled gratefully.

Andrea smiled back at her.

"I'm going to make breakfast for mom. Do you want anything?"

"No, thank you. I think I'm gonna go lie down for a bit," Julia replied, pushing away from the island.

"Okay, sweetie. I hope you feel better soon."

With one final smile, Julia turned and headed out of the kitchen. Andrea turned to the refrigerator removing the ingredients to make her mom a shake and a simple breakfast of mashed potato omelet. Since Becky's ALS made it to stage two, her symptoms had been progressing rapidly. Currently, she barely had functionality in her right hand, her mobility on hold was slowly going as well as her speech and swallowing solid foods had become increasingly difficult. Sooner than later, they were going to have to feed her intravenously. She sighed solemnly. Sometimes it proved to be too much just to think about the future— to face the inevitable.

After everything was set up, she placed them on a tray and walked across the hall to the bedroom Becky was currently occupying. Balancing the tray in one arm, she knocked on the door twice before turning the knob and using her shoulder blade to push it open.

"Good morning, Mom," she greeted Becky with the brightest smile she could muster.

Becky's lips upturned in a small smile as she tried to raise herself into a sitting position.

"Wait, let me help you." Andrea rushed to place the tray on the overbed table and put her hands under Becky's arms, supporting the weight to lift her up in the bed. When she was situated. Andrea used the levers to bring the bed up so that her mother's back was almost at a ninety degree angle.

"Th-th-thank y-you s-s-sweeeetheaart."

"You're welcome," Andrea replied cheerily, even as bands of sadness tightened across her chest. "Ready to eat?"

"Mhmm," Becky replied.

Andrea used the spoon to scoop up some of the semi-solid mash and brought it to her mother's lips. Becky took the spoon into her mouth before the food slowly disappeared. Andrea watched her carefully, noting the faraway look in her dull brown eyes.

"Are you all right, Mom?"

Becky turned to her daughter with a small, sad smile. "I w-wa-was th...thinking of y-your father."

Andrea nodded in understanding. "I miss him too," she said, voicing what her mother couldn't. Her mother looked down at her frail hands, which seemed to have shrunk to half their original size since Andrea returned. She wanted to bring Becky closer, to hug her tightly and never let go, but she knew that would only lead to her bursting into tears, and that would, in turn, sadden her mother. She didn't want that. Becky was already suffering enough as it was.

"I know dad is pleased that we get to spend this time with you. Nothing mattered as much to him as your happiness," she spoke soothingly.

This time Becky's lips upturned in gratitude. Andrea reached over to place a kiss against her temple before resuming feeding her. Just as she finished, Cora popped in and took over.

After making a shake for herself, Andrea left for the inn. she remembered Marg had mentioned wanting her input on the lounge area she was planning to set up for their guests to use to complete whatever work they would have taken with them. However, just as she was about to enter the lobby, Ben stepped through the door holding Marg close to his side while she held her right hand loosely in her left hand as it rested against her chest. From the look on her face and the way she grimaced with each step, it was obvious she was in pain.

"What happened?" Andrea asked in alarm.

"I fell and hit my hand against the edge of the reception desk," Marg replied.

"I'm taking her to the emergency room," Ben added immediately after.

"Of course, go, go," Andrea responded on alert mode. "Don't worry. I'll handle the front desk," she informed them.

"Thanks, Drea," Marg replied gratefully, even as she winced in pain.

"No need to thank me, Marg. Now go," she responded, all but pushing them toward the parking lot.

"I'll let you know how it went," Marg called back as Ben ushered her away.

For the next couple of hours, Andrea spent the time going over the reservations calendar and updating the guest list.

"Thanks for making Willberry Inn a part of your experience here at Oak Harbor. I hope you had a wonderful time and hope to see you again." Andrea smiled as she delivered the inn's signature farewell speech to the lovely couple standing before her as they checked out.

"Thanks. We had a great time here, and we'll definitely be heading back here," the female with light brown hair replied as the man at her side continued to stare affectionately at her.

A smile played at Andrea's lips as she noted how the gentleman stared at the woman, the more bashful she became.

"Enjoy the rest of your honeymoon."

"Oh, we plan to. Trust me. The man replied with a glint in his eyes as she stared at his wife, whose cheeks had become noticeably red.

After the couple left, Andrea decided to head up to the second floor to the room they had been occupying. The room, like almost all the others in the inn, was simple and old-fashioned, maintaining the authenticity of the colonial architecture. She quickly stripped the bed of the sheets and duvet and brought them down to the washroom. The assistant they'd hired after promoting Marg to Assistant Manager would come in later to clean and prepare the room for occupancy by a future guest.

Just as she exited the washroom and headed for the reception area, Ben and Marg appeared, the latter sporting a cast over her wrist and part way up her forearm.

"Is it broken?" she asked worriedly.

"It's a small hairline fracture. I'm okay. The doctor says I should keep the cast on to keep it from straining too much while it heals.

"Oh, okay. I'm happy it wasn't more than that," Andrea responded, relieved.

"Yeah. Me too. What happened while I was away?" she asked.

"Oh, not much. A few of our guests have gone in the town, a couple checked out, and three more are scheduled to check out by the end of this week.

"That's good. When are Rory's guests scheduled to arrive?"

"The week after Thanksgiving," Andrea informed her.

"Good. By then, all our current guests will have checked out," Marg responded, nodding her head contemplatively.

"Have you made any plans for Thanksgiving?" Andrea asked.

Marg looked over at Ben, her eyes shining bright as a smile graced her lips.

"Ben asked me to share Thanksgiving with him and his children," Marg informed her.

"Oh," Andrea responded, turning her questioning gaze at Ben. "I thought you were coming over for Thanksgiving."

Ben gave her a sheepish smile as he scratched the back of his neck. "I'm sorry about that, Drea. I just wanted to have a small, private Thanksgiving with her and the kids so that they could get to know each other more," he replied apologetically.

"Why don't we have our little private Thanksgiving a little earlier and then go over to the family gathering? Kill two birds with one stone." Marg suggested.

"That's not a bad idea," Ben agreed.

"It's fine if you guys can't make it. You deserve this time together," Andrea assured them.

"Thanks, Drea," Marg spoke, her tone full of gratitude.

"Not a problem."

After another couple of hours, staying to help Marg, Andrea left for the main house to prepare for her date with Donny.

Chapter Seventeen

Andrea stared at her reflection in the mirror. Her light brown hair lay flat against her head. She wasn't sure how she wanted it.

There was a knock at her door followed by, "Mom?"

"Come in, sweetie," she invited her daughter.

Andrea turned to Rory, her lips downturned like a lost puppy.

"Up or down?" she asked, using her hands to swoop her hair up in one before releasing it to fall back in place against her head.

Rory tapped her chin contemplatively before replying, "Up. It'll bring more attention to your face, especially your eyes...you have really pretty eyes."

Andrea cheesed. "You sure know how to boost my confidence when I need it," she praised.

"I try," Rory replied with a smug shrug of her shoulders before bursting into laughter, her mother joining in.

She turned to get the brush to smooth out her hair.

"Let me help you," Rory offered.

"Thanks," she replied gratefully. She held the brush out to her daughter, who took it. Andrea sat on the ottoman before the vanity, allowing Rory to start brushing and detangling. After applying mousse to her hair, Rory brought it upward before securing it in position with a clip. After snapping it shut, she used the brush to brush the strands as they spilled from the teeth of the clip down her nape to rest just a little way below her shoulders.

"Have you decided on the dress you're wearing?" Rory asked after she finished fluffing her mother's hair.

"I did," Andrea confirmed. "It's hanging from the closet door.

Rory walked over to it. At her sharp intake of breath, Andrea turned to her.

"This dress is beautiful," her daughter gushed, looking from the gown to her.

"I'm almost certain Donny will be speechless when he sees you."

Andrea's cheeks warmed, and her lips, of their own accord, turned up in a smile.

"Help me put it on?" she requested.

Rory lifted the wine-red, one-shoulder, scuba midi dress with an exaggerated frill in the front. It was truly a remarkable piece.

After Rory brought the side zipper in place, Andrea turned to the mirror to once again stare at her reflection. She was wearing the bare minimum of makeup, just light blush to highlight her cheekbones, burgundy lipstick and some eyeliner to add more detail to her already striking blue eyes. The dress fit her like a glove, accentuating her lithe physique.

"You look stunning," her daughter complimented.

Andrea wasn't vain, but she had to admit that she did look really good in the dress, and for that reason, she stared appreciatively at herself a little longer than she normally did. She smiled in anticipation of Donny's reaction when he finally saw her.

After adding some silver, drop earrings and strappy black stilettos, she was ready.

"Wow, sis, you look really beautiful," Cora expressed the second she walked into the den, where the rest of the family sat watching TV.

"Donny's going to short circuit," Jo smirked.

"I see I have been a bad influence on my poor innocent little sister," Andrea joked. Her eyes darted over to her mom, who sat with her feet stretched out before her on an ottoman and cushions behind her, propping her up. Becky's eyes shone with approval. Just then, the doorbell rang.

"I'll get it," Rory jumped up.

Two minutes later, she entered the room with a clean-shaven Donny, sporting a gray blazer over a navy sweater over a white dress shirt tucked into black slacks and charcoal moccasins. His dirty blond hair was shaved at the sides, and the hair on top swept to the back. He looked like a man who belonged on the cover of a men's magazine.

Donny's eyes widened at her before his sharp blue eyes smiled warmly down at her.

"You look...you're breathtaking," he managed to say.

Andrea's cheeks burned as they flashed crimson.

"These are for you," he said, lifting the bouquet of flowers she hadn't noticed before.

"Thank you," she replied demurely, accepting the arrangement of orange and red roses and pink tulips. She brought them up to her nose and inhaled deeply. "They're lovely," she replied, smiling at him.

"I'm glad you like them," he said, his piercing gaze never leaving her.

"All right, guys, save some for the actual date," Cora called out jokingly.

Andrea stepped back and stared at her family with a sheepish expression. She'd forgotten they were there.

After greeting the rest of the women in the house, Donny directed her to his parked SUV, and soon they were sailing down the highway, giddy and expectant.

"Where are we going?" Andrea asked him for the third time in the last half hour.

"It's a surprise," Donny repeated, glancing at her with mischief dancing in his eyes before focusing on the road again.

"I hate surprises," Andrea pouted.

"That's what you always say, but you always turn out pleased by them," Donny chuckled.

Andrea huffed and folded her arms across her chest. "Well, I don't like this surprise then," she spoke matter of factly.

"You'll enjoy it. I promise," Donny said reassuringly.

Andrea stared out the window at the passing trees, cars, and streetlights as they continued driving further north. Soon they entered Skagit County, causing Andrea to look over at him curiously.

"We're going to Anacortes," he informed her.

Ten minutes later, they pulled up to a building that looked more like an auditorium, but when they entered, the establishment was well decorated, from the plush carpeted floors to the high ceilings and chandelier in the center of the room. It was a magnificent setup.

After checking her coat, they followed the maître d to their seat.

"Have I told you how lovely you look this evening?" Donny asked her the minute the waitress left them alone. His glittering blue eyes shone with appreciation and something else entirely. Andrea felt her pulse quicken and her throat suddenly felt parched. Reaching for the glass of water, she took a considerable drink, grateful for the liquid bringing back moisture to her drying inside as it made its path toward her stomach.

"This place is amazing and so worth the mystery," she spoke appreciatively, glancing around the fancy establishment before staring back at Donny with a mischievous glint. "It's almost as great as how handsome you look tonight," she smirked at him. Now it was his turn to feel like a deer caught in headlights. Donny reached for his own water glass and took a large drink.

"Well played," he grinned when he finally regained his composure to find his voice.

"Take note, I play to win," she stated with an earsplitting grin.

"Is that so?" Donny returned before adding, "touché," lifting the glass and tipping it in her direction as if to say, "Challenge accepted."

The waiter arrived at that moment with their first course. As dinner progressed, the two settled into a routine of who could make the other blush more or feel more pushed into the spotlight. It ended with them having a great laugh.

"I really enjoy spending time with you," Donny looked up to say, his expression mirroring his words.

Andrea smiled affectionately. "I enjoy spending time with you too," she affirmed, her smarting cheeks brightening again. "And right now, since we've skipped a few steps on our date so far, let's rewind a bit," she suggested.

Donny's brows came together, a look of confusion clouding his features. "What do you mean?" he asked.

"I should have commented on how lovely the weather is even though it was almost freezing outside, then I should have asked how your day was..." she trailed off.

Donny guffawed. "You are just full of surprises," he quipped. "I had a good day. I went to work; we were called out to a building that had excessive smoke coming from one of the rooms. Turns out a plug short-circuited. Oh, and I helped deliver a baby."

Andrea's hand flew to her mouth, covering the o her lips made at him, retelling how his day at work went. "The life of a firefighter is truly an eventful one," she commented. "I really appreciated all the work that you and your team do for the community," she complimented, reaching across the table to squeeze his hand encouragingly.

Donny flipped his palm over to connect with hers and intertwine their fingers.

"Looks like I need to talk about my job more to gain brownie points," he surmised with a grin. "But you know...I love what I do, and I have an amazing team behind me that I really appreciate and love. They're my family, you know," he spoke seriously.

Andrea nodded her understanding.

"I almost forgot. They told me to tell you hello and that they miss you coming around the station."

"Aww, I miss them too," she replied. "It's been a busy couple of weeks with mom, the inn, Rory, but I promise I'll make time to go hangout with them."

Donny squeezed her palm and locked his gaze with hers.

"It's okay if you can't make it now, Drea. The guys understand," he said seriously.

She nodded in understanding. "Just know that I expect my own locker with my own gear when I come back," she smirked.

"Yes, ma'am," Donny saluted with his free hand, his blue eyes bright with laughter.

"Desert is served," the waiter announced as he approached their table. He placed Andrea's coffee cookie crumble before her and Donny's tiramisu before him.

"Thank you," they both replied.

After the waiter left, she dug into the sweet treat, the rich coffee taste and the texture filling her with satisfaction. A soft moan of approval left her lips and her eyes closed as she savored the taste. When she opened her eyes, Donny was staring at her in awe.

"This cake is really spectacular," she expressed, pulling a piece onto the fork, and holding it out to him. Donny leaned forward to accept her cake. After a few chews, his head bobbed in approval.

"You're right. It's great," he agreed.

Andrea smiled approvingly before returning her attention to her dessert. "How's Bruce and Janice?"

"They're fine," Donny responded in between bites of his own dessert. "I spoke to them yesterday. Janice had an ultrasound, and my grandson is a healthy ball of energy." He beamed with pride.

"That's great news," Andrea replied, pleased.

After a few more talks about their children, Donny finally asked for the check.

The two walked hand in hand toward Donny's car. Andrea was grateful for the extra warmth their connected palms provided. Even though she had on her tweed jacket, the biting cold still seeped through, making her a bit chilly. She noted it was considerably colder at this end of the island than it was back in Oak Harbor.

Donny turned on the heater the moment he started up the car, a welcome reprieve for her.

Andrea looked over at him while he drove. He turned to her, his look questioning before his eyes were front and center once more.

"In case I don't get to tell you. I had a wonderful time tonight," she informed him.

A smile graced his lips. Without taking his eyes off the road, he reached for her hand across the console and joined their fingers. "I had a really good time too," he confirmed. She leaned over to rest her head on his shoulder as a smile of contentment settled on her lips. However, that contentment quickly disappeared into alarm at the blaring red lights coming from the main house, putting her on high alert. She exchanged a worried look with Donny.

As soon as his car stopped right behind the ambulance parked right at the porch steps, Andrea rushed out, her heart beating wildly. An ambulance here could only mean one thing — her mom. She froze in place when she saw the stretcher pass through the open door, but her petrification quickly turned to confusion when she saw Cora holding the hand of a crying Julia as the paramedic wheeled her out.

"What happened?" Andrea asked the minute she got to them.

Cora glanced at her, but no words came from her mouth. The look on her sister's face knifed through Andrea.

"Ma'am, we gotta move now," the paramedic advised. Cora looked from Julia to her, her expression helpless.

"Go," Andrea encouraged. Everything will be okay. Cora followed them up in the van that closed immediately after she sat, and right after, the van hurtled down the pathway, the siren announcing that they had an emergency case.

Andrea turned back to the door to see her daughter standing with her hand across her chest, a helpless expression on her face. "What happened?"

Her question seemed to snap Rory out of her stupor as she turned to focus on her. "Aunt Cora found her on the bathroom floor...she was doubled over in pain and...and bleeding."

Andrea's heart slammed against her chest. She felt a soothing hand against her back and looked up to see Donny staring back at her in concern. A wave of guilt flooded her.

She should have said something to Cora this morning.

Chapter Eighteen

Rory wiped at the tear that had escaped to fall down her cheek as the final credits of the movie she'd been watching with her family began rolling. It had been a good movie, but it had a bitter-sweet ending.

"I thought they would have ended up together," she heard her aunt say from beside her with melancholy.

"Me too," her mother agreed from her other side. Rory looked over to see Andrea swiping at the tears that were falling over each other as they cascaded down her flushed face.

A rueful smile graced her lips as Rory nodded her agreement, unable to voice her own sentiments, even though it had been touted as a romance movie, the main characters, although madly in love, in the end, chose different paths that led them away from each other. Sometimes love really wasn't enough, and people ended up fighting a battle that they would eventually lose. However, love also made letting go difficult. Her mind flashed to James, and her heart squeezed tightly against her chest.

She wished she knew...

"Are you all right, sweetie?"

Shaking her head to clear her thoughts, she looked over at her mother with a small smile of assurance. "I'm okay. This movie just really got to me."

Andrea nodded in understanding, but concern stirred behind her blue eyes.

The doorbell sounded from the hall, filling the house with its musical chimes.

"I'll get it," Rory volunteered, rising from the couch, and walking toward the hall.

"Oh, hi, Cousin Tessa. Hi Dianne," Rory greeted the two women standing at the open door.

"Hi, sweetie. You know you can just call me Tessa; I won't be offended. I promise," Tessa said, reaching forward to hug her.

"Force of habit," Rory expressed, leaning forward as Tessa's arms warmly embraced her.

"Hey, Rory," Dianne greeted when they separated, reaching over to hug her as well.

"Are your mother and aunts here?" Tessa asked.

"Um, yeah. They're in the family room. We were watching a movie." She led them down the hall.

"Hi, ladies," Tessa's greeted the sisters cheerily the moment she stepped into the family room.

"Hi, Tessa," they greeted back, each rising to embrace her and Dianne.

"Did...did you see Jules?" Cora tentatively asks.

"Not since last night when she came in," Tessa answered, giving her an apology.

"Oh, okay," Cora responded, her voice low and disappointed.

"What's wrong? Did you get bad news?"

"No, no. The doctor says everything's fine. Nothing new to

report. We need to eliminate any stressors for Jules because it's not good for the baby," Cora explained.

Tessa's chin jerked in agreement. "So, she'll be on bed rest," she surmised.

Cora nodded, yes. "I've been calling her cell, but it goes straight to voicemail," she revealed with a collapse of her shoulders.

"I'm sure it's nothing, Cora. She's probably just resting," Andrea spoke up.

"I know," Cora responded with a purse of her lips.

"When is she being discharged?" Tessa asked.

"Today. I'm leaving within the hour to pick her up.".

Rory stood by the wall watching the conversation between the older women when a hand waved before her face.

"Hey."

She turned to look at Dianne questioningly.

"I'm going over to the Camano Islands. They have a wine tasting at the Kristoferson Farm. Would you like to go with me?"

"Yeah. Of course," Rory jumped at the opportunity to visit one of the other islands of Puget Sound.

"Great," Dianne clapped. "I just need to ask Cora if we can borrow the boat."

"Okay."

Rory watched as Dianne made her way over to Aunt Cora. Her phone vibrating in the front of her shorts caught her attention, and she reached inside her pocket to get it. Her eyes squinted at the number on the screen.

"Hello?"

"Hi, Rory, it's Trey."

"Oh, hi, Trey. How are you?"

"I'm good. How are you?"

"I'm okay," she answered.

"Listen, I was wondering if you're free. We could maybe hang out. We could catch a movie or something."

"I'm sorry, Trey, as great as that sounds, I just promised my cousin that I'd go with her over to Camano Island," she said apologetically.

"Oh...no, that's fine. I understand."

Rory felt a pang at the disappointment in his voice, but just then an idea popped into her head.

"You could come with us if you want. I could ask Dianne...I don't think she'd mind," she offered.

"I don't know..."

"Oh, come on, Trey. It'll be fun," she coaxed. "Here's Dianne now. I'm asking her."

"Ask me what?" Dianne asked as she stopped before Rory and stared questioningly.

Rory moved the phone away from her ear as she asked, "Can Trey, mom's soon-to-be stepson, come with us?"

"Yeah. Of course," she agreed.

Rory threw her cousin a thumbs up before returning to the call. "You're coming with us," she said definitively.

"Okay...then," Trey responded, unsure of what just happened.

"How fast can you get here?"

"About twenty minutes?"

"Good. See you then. Bye."

Rory turned to Dianne with a bright smile on her lips. "Is there a dress code?" she asked, taking in her cousin's not-so-casual outfit of a cream cashmere turtleneck tucked into a pair of gray jeans and black low-heeled ankle boots.

"No, not really," Dianne replied, looking her up and down. "Just wear something comfortable. They have ziplining at the farm in case you want to do that."

"Really?" Rory asked, surprised. "I'd definitely want to do that. Let me head upstairs and get changed really quick."

"Okay," Diane agreed.

Rory left her mother and aunts talking to Tessa and made her way upstairs to change. After rummaging through her closet, she settled on a simple white t-shirt with black leggings and some Ugg boots. Finally, she reached for her hoodie jean jacket and slung it over her arm and returned downstairs. Only Diane was in the family room when she returned.

"Where are the others?"

"Your mother is sitting with Aunt Becky, and the others are out back."

Rory nodded. "You know, I think Trey would like the idea of ziplining," she contemplated. It was a great idea to have invited him. A smile appeared on her lips. she looked up and caught Dianne's perceptive gaze. "What?"

"It's nothing," she replied, flicking her wrist forward in a nonchalant fashion.

"It's nothing," Rory countered. "That look was saying something."

"I was just thinking... it's refreshing to see you guys getting along, that's all," she reasoned.

Rory smiled at her cousin and nodded. "It's surprising how quickly we settled our differences, but I understand him better now, and I'm able to see that he's a really down-to-earth guy and cool to hang out with. It's starting to feel like I'm gaining a brother— two brothers actually, from my mom's relationship with Donny, and I'm glad, especially getting to spend time doing fun things with him like this."

Dianne tipped her head in understanding, but her lips twitched downward as a shadow of regret passed over her face. "I know what you mean. I kinda wished me and Jake still did stuff like that."

"Why don't you guys?" Rory asked.

Dianne's hazel eyes were doleful as she replied. "We used to do everything together. We were inseparable, you didn't see one of us without the other being close by, but ever since our dad died two years ago, he's been...different— distant. It feels like we've grown even farther apart since I got engaged." Her eyes shifted to the ground as she mumbled, "It's like I don't exist to him anymore."

"That's not true, Dianne." She reached over and rubbed her arm encouragingly. "I'm sure the same Jake you used to do all those things with is still there. He's just...trying to find a way to cope with all the changes he's had to go through. He still needs you, even if he doesn't say it."

The doorbell sounded, halting the rest of her speech. "That must be Trey. I'll get it." Rory rose, turned, and made her way toward the front door. She pulled it open to see him standing before her with his hands in the pockets of the blue hoodie pullover he was wearing, a broad grin on his face. Instantly her own lips lifted to mimic his.

"Hey, you," she greeted.

"Hey," he greeted, stepping through the door. "So, why exactly are we going to Camano Island?" he asked, looking down at her.

"We're going to a wine tasting," she replied.

Trey's brows scrunched together. "A what?" he asked.

"Wine. Tasting." she enunciated.

A frown etched into the corner of his mouth.

A bubble of laughter erupted from Rory at his expression. "It'll be fun," she persuaded, hooking her arm with his, effectively preventing him from escaping. She walked him down the hall toward the family room. "Don't worry, we're doing more than just wine tasting," she assured him.

"Like what?" he asked, a brow raised in skepticism.

"They have ziplining," she said excitedly.

This got Trey's attention. "Are we going to the Kristofersons' Farm?"

"Yup," she confirmed with a quick nod.

"Sweet," Trey expressed, his mood improving.

"Trey, you remember Dianne?" she asked when they finally stepped into the room.

"Hi, Dianne," he greeted with a slight wave.

Dianne returned his wave while giving him a polite smile. "Hi." She turned to Rory. "Ready to go?"

The trio left the house and made their way down to the dock. It was almost noon, but the sun barely peaked through the silver clouds. The slightly gusty wind swirled around them. The brilliantly colored fallen leaves rolled over each other, some levitating above the earth as they followed the rhythm of the wind. It was really chilly. Rory slipped on her jacket.

When they made it to the dock, Diane untied the boat while Trey climbed aboard and reached out to help Rory onto the deck.

"All aboard!" Dianne called out gleefully. "I've always wanted to say that," she finished with a small fist pump.

Rory chuckled at her cousin's silliness before settling in the cockpit with Trey. Dianne, who was now standing at the helm, guided the boat out of the harbor, leaving a trail of smooth wave pool tides as the engine revved.

As the boat glided effortlessly through the blue-green waters, Rory and Trey rose from the seats to lean over the railing at the side, looking out at the horizon. The cold water spritzed their faces as the chilly offshore breeze became gustier. Rory could see a few birds in the distance soaring high. The snowcapped mountain ranges in the distance and the cloud-filled sky resembled a canvas set in place. She felt relaxed, peaceful.

Twenty minutes later, the boat coasted its way to the small inlet at Barnum Bay.

"The farm is a fifteen minutes' walk from here," Dianne informed them, leading the way up the shore. The trio made their way toward the town.

When they finally made it to the farm, Rory was completely bowled over. From what she could already see, the large, colonial-style farmhouse was completely surrounded by farmed plots and bordered by evergreens and edges.

"Hi. Welcome to K farm. I'm Kim. Are you here for the wine tasting or ziplining?" a brunette with a bright smile welcomed.

"We're here for both," Dianne spoke up.

"Excellent," she replied with a smile. "You'll need these," she held out some square papers to them.

They reached for the sheets and scanned them.

"This is a list of the wines and a description of the aging process for you to have a better understanding and appreciation of the tasting," Kim further explained.

"Is this real? This wine is over eighty years old?" Trey looked back at the woman seriously as he pointed to one of the wines on the list.

"That is correct," Kim affirmed. "Not only is it very old, but it is an original product of this farm," she finished proudly.

"That's cool," Trey nodded his head.

"May I have your IDs to verify your ages? We can't serve alcohol to anyone under twenty-one," Kim informed them.

At this, Trey's face fell.

Rory snickered. "Look at the bright side Trey. You still have ziplining."

"Yeah. Whatever," he replied, annoyed.

Rory couldn't help the laughter that bubbled to the surface as she watched her soon-to-be stepbrother sulk over something he hadn't been enthused about in the first place.

They were going to have a lot of fun today; she was sure of it.

Chapter Nineteen

"Hi, sweetie. How was your time out with Dianne and Trey?"

"Hi, Mom." Rory planted a kiss on Andrea's cheek and walked around her. "It was great. I had a lot of fun," she replied, opening the refrigerator and poking her head inside. She reached for a can of soda.

Andrea stopped stirring the pot that sat on the stove to look over at her daughter. "And Trey?"

Rory straightened and turned to her mother, who was staring expectantly back at her. "He had fun, too," she smirked.

"Rory, you know I'm asking for more than that," her mother pressed.

"We got along, Mom. He talked a lot about his dad and…"

Andrea's head slowly dipped, her chin almost touching her chest as she looked over at her daughter hopefully.

"He said he likes you a lot. You're really nice, and he thinks you're good for Donny."

Andrea's face broke out into a broad smile. "He really said that?"

Rory nodded, her face breaking out in a smile. "Trust me, Mom. If Donny was going to propose to you right now, you won't get any objections— at least not from Trey," she assured her.

Surprise danced in Andrea's eyes as she took a step back. "Who said anything about a proposal...wait, did he say his father is planning to propose? I-I-we...but..." Andrea's words faltered. She looked at her daughter with dread. "I'm not ready...we're not ready."

Rory held up her hands to calm her mother. "Mom, relax. Trey didn't say anything about Donny planning to propose. I was just saying he wouldn't object to it."

Andrea's shoulders relaxed as she breathed a sigh of relief.

"It wouldn't be a bad thing, though. I think you guys would make a wonderful couple," Rory voiced her opinion.

"It's too soon. We've only been dating for a little over five months," Andrea reasoned.

Rory fixed her gaze on her mother. "Mom, it doesn't matter how long you've known him. If you love him and he loves you and can see a future with you, then that's all that should matter."

Andrea opened her mouth to say something, but Rory beat her to it.

"Do you love him?"

She hesitated before answering, "I do."

"And do you think he loves you?"

Her definitive answer once again was, "I do," she sighed. She turned and extinguished the flame under the stew before turning back to look at her daughter as she spoke, "But I do not think we're ready to be married," she stressed. "I don't know if I want to be married," she said just above a whisper, her voice raw with vulnerability.

Rory walked up to Andrea and took her hands in hers. "I know you're scared, Mom, and I get it. You think you need more time before taking that big step, and that's understandable. It's just...I've seen how your face lights up when you talk about him, and I've witnessed how much he cares for you and how sensitive he is to your feelings and emotions. Sometimes I wish..." she didn't finish the statement, but sometimes she wished that James could be that aware of her feelings. She wished he realized just how much she needed him, missed him — without her having to say the words. "You deserve to be happy, Mom...more than anyone I know. I believe that when Donny does ask, it'll be the right time. Just...be open to the idea."

Andrea smiled appreciatively at her daughter. She reached up to cup Rory's cheek lovingly. "What did I do to deserve a daughter like you?"

Rory felt the warmth creep up the sides of her neck before her face became warm, and her lips turned up into a smile.

"I'm gonna head upstairs and take a shower," she informed her mother when they separated.

"Okay, sweetie. Dinner should be ready by the time you're done."

Rory nodded and headed for the door but stopped and whipped around. "Did Aunt Cora pick Jules up from the hospital?"

"Yes. She's in her room, but she's resting. She ate earlier," Andrea informed her.

"Okay. I'm just happy that she's back home," Rory expressed.

"Me too," Andrea smiled, agreeing.

Rory made it to her room and took a quick, warm shower. Just as she stepped out of the bathroom, her phone began vibrating. Securing the towel around her, she launched herself across the bed, flopping on her belly as she reached for the device.

"Hello?" she answered as soon as she hit the answer button.

"Hi."

Her heart skipped a beat, and her pulse quickened. "Hi," she softly breathed out, flipping onto her back.

"Hi," he repeated. After a short pause, he added, "are you busy? You sound out of breath."

"I was in the shower," she responded, her eyes glued to the ceiling.

"Oh...okay."

There was another pregnant pause.

"What are you doing?" she broke the silence.

"I'm at this silly, boring fundraising with Mom and Dad. I stepped out for a bit to call you. I really wish you were here."

"Why?" Rory heard herself ask.

"Because I miss you," James replied almost immediately.

"Miss me, how?" Rory's brows scrunched together in confusion. She wasn't sure why she was pushing the issue, but something inside her was telling her she needed to get answers.

"What's that supposed to mean?" James' question broke into her inner thought.

Rory sighed tiredly. "Do you still have the prenup?"

There was another long pause before James replied, "I do."

Rory shook her head, and her lips turned downward. "You know how I feel about it and the fact that it was your mother who came up with it, and yet...you miss me," she said, her voice hollow.

"Rory," James breathed out frustratedly. "I didn't call to fight with you tonight—"

"Is that what we're doing?" she interrupted. "Fighting?"

"Rory, I love you. Why can't that be enough?" he quipped.

Her face fell even more. "I've come to realize that this time apart was important, and I'm happy I did it."

"Rory...I miss you, I do. Please just come home," James pleaded. "We can't work this out so far apart."

The break in his voice tore at her heart. She almost caved.

"Tell me something, James...why do you still have the prenup?"

Her fiancé breathed out heavily before responding, "I don't know."

"And that James is precisely why I can't come home," she spoke solemnly. With a defeated sigh of her own, she continued, "You need to use the time to choose the future you want... one with me in it or one without me."

"How did we get here?" James asked.

"I don't know what to tell you, James...All I know is you need to figure it out. Until then, I'll be here. I have to go. Bye."

Rory immediately terminated the call and allowed the phone to slip through her hand to land on the bed. She stared unseeing at the ceiling. Her chest felt hollow, and her heart had slowed so much so that it could possibly be described as a kneeling church bell, and her body felt heavy with sadness. *How had they gotten here?*

"Rory, honey, dinner's ready."

"I'll be there in a little while Aunt Jo. Thanks," she called out to her aunt, who was standing on the other side of the closed door.

Rory swiped at the single tear that slithered down her cheek and dragged herself out of bed. After getting dressed, she went downstairs to have dinner with her family.

* * *

"I was thinking...since Thanksgiving is only a week away, why don't we start decorating for the holiday? What do you think about putting a faux pumpkin garland around the door frame and maybe some along the staircase banisters? We could even hang a pampas grass wreath on the front door too and have some colorful fall plants and pumpkins lining the edges of the porch steps."

Marg inclined her head in consideration of Rory's suggestions. A smile broke out on her face as she fixed her gaze on her. "That's a great idea, Rory. I can see it already. I know our guests will appreciate the effort to make them feel at home."

"That's what I was going for," Rory revealed lowly.

Marg smiled appreciatively. "You really have a knack for this," she complimented.

"That she does," Andrea chipped in, smiling proudly at her daughter.

Rory's cheeks felt stiff from how much she had been smiling since arriving at the inn to help her mother and Marg because the receptionist they'd hired recently had come down with a stomach bug.

"Maybe we could add some garden gnomes and some bales of hay around the lawn too."

"That could definitely work," Marg agreed with her suggestions. "The Target downtown would definitely have these."

"Now would be a good time to go purchase them," Andrea thought out loud. "You should definitely buy them today."

"Yeah, but with Abigail out, there's nobody to man the reception desk," Marg countered.

"I can man the reception desk until you get back," Rory stepped in.

"Are you sure?" Marg asked hesitantly.

"Yeah, go. I don't mind. Plus, Mom will be close if I run into any problems while you're away."

"That's right. I'll be in my office all day. If she needs help, I'm just right down the hall," Andrea confirmed.

"All right. I'm gonna go. I need to pick up some ointment for the rash on my elbow," Marg spoke, raising her casted forearm to show them the red splotches at the back of her arm just above the top of the cast.

"You definitely need to take care of that," Andrea voiced her concern.

Marg inclined her head in agreement. "Thanks again, Rory. You're a Godsend," she smiled at her.

Rory returned the smile.

After Marg left for Target, Andrea returned to her office in the back and Rory stationed herself behind the reception desk. Within fifteen minutes of being there, Rory had greeted seven of the nine guests that currently occupied six of the eight guest rooms. She'd made suggestions to two couples who wanted to go out to dinner later in the evening, giving them a rundown of the ones she'd been, and she'd even suggested that one of the guests who'd wanted something a little more exhilarating than hiking and water sports that he could try ziplining on the Kristofersens' farm.

By the time an hour had passed, she'd interacted with eight of the guests. Just as she was settling down to take up the latest Daniel Steel novel she'd been reading, a man and a woman came through the open door. They looked pretty young, but what caught Rory was how they couldn't take their eyes off each other and how bright their smiles were that seemed a permanent trait. Then she noticed the female's hand on the man's chest; it sported a huge rock on her ring finger.

"Hi, welcome to Willberry Inn and property," Rory greeted with a bright smile.

"Thank you. We made a reservation under Mr. and Mrs. Flemmings," the woman replied cheerily. Her husband offered Rory a cursory nod and polite smile before his eyes were back on his wife, shining with affection.

"We're newlyweds. We didn't want to do the hotels or resorts...been there, done that, you know?"

Rory nodded her head in understanding as she listened to the woman.

"We just wanted to have our honeymoon where we can get

to focus on each other while still enjoying the ambiance of a beautiful town. We just got here, and we already love it."

"Wonderful," Rory responded. "Oak Harbor is truly a magical place. I'm sure you'll love all of it."

The woman smiled appreciatively.

"Okay, let's see...here we are. Mr. and Mrs. Flemmings, you are booked for room eight, it's on the last floor. I'd be happy to help you guys get settled," Rory offered, but the couple had already gone back into their own bubble; whatever her husband had whispered in her ears caused Mr. Flemings to giggle, her cheeks flushing red.

A wave of longing came over Rory at their open display of affection, and her mind flashed to James.

"We'll take it from here, but thanks for your help," The man turned to say to Rory.

"Okay. Here you go." She placed the key for the room in his outstretched hand. She watched them walk arm in arm up the stairs, Mrs. Flemmings' giggles filling the hall as they slowly disappeared from view.

She decided to take a break, then put up the sign to ring for assistance and made her way out toward the back patio. The sky was a bleak gray tone, devoid of any of its usual blue and so reflective of her mood. She was pretty sure that the rain would follow soon, as the temperature had also dropped even further. Rory pulled her sweater closer around her. Her cell vibrated in her pant pocket. A wave of nausea washed over her at the name on the screen. Slowly she brought it up to her ear.

"Hi, Lenora. So nice to hear from you," she greeted as pleasantly as she could muster.

"Hello, Aurora. I can't say the same, but I will get straight to the point."

Rory's heart dropped to the bottom of her stomach.

"Are you planning on jilting my son at the altar?"

Chapter Twenty

"Lenora, why would you think that?"
"It's been almost a month! The wedding is only a month away, and yet I have not heard a peep out of you," Lenora spoke, her tone boiling.

"Everything is under control," Rory replied calmly while her heart beat erratically against her rib cage and her breathing became shallower.

"It's like you're deliberately trying to cut us out of the wedding. You haven't cared to let me know how far along you are with the planning. For all I know, we'll be sitting on hay bales and eating and drinking from disposable plates and cups."

Rory pinched the bridge of her nose as her eyes squeezed shut. Her chest rose and fell rapidly while she tried to calm herself and not react to her mother-in-law's insults.

"Lenora, I told you this before, Jenny, my wedding planner, has everything under control. She's flying in after Thanksgiving to personally view the venue and make her final preparations. Also, my mom and I have already chosen my wedding dress in Seattle, the cake is taken care of, and the caterers and florists have been contracted," she listed, making sure that the woman realized that without her help, she'd pulled it off.

"And you didn't care to say any of this to me? You've already cut me out of making any meaningful suggestions or additions to this wedding, and yet you didn't feel the need to let me know what was happening," Lenora responded, her voice full of judgment.

Rory shook her head slowly as an exasperated breath released from her lips. What had she done to deserve this woman in her life?

"Look, Lenora, I'm sorry I didn't call you to give you an update on the wedding; that's on me, but the wedding is taking place here in Oak Harbor and not the city, which means I have been hyper-focused on having everything in place before the date and I am not cutting you out of the wedding...it's just that your earlier suggestions are not in line with the theme that I have in mind," she tried to explain even as her patience wore thin.

The sharp hiss of breath that only occurred by the locking of teeth and a sharp release of air coming through the speaker caused Rory to remove the phone from her ear to look to see that it was the same sophisticated, high society Lenora she was speaking to before placing it back at her ear.

"And what about my son, hmm?"

"What about James?" Rory tiredly asked.

There was a short pause before the woman spoke again, "It seems to me that my son does not have a say in this wedding at all. It's all about you and what you want."

"That's not true, Lenora," Rory refuted, her anger rising to the surface once more. "James has as much of a say as I do, and he knows that," she defended.

"And yet...he's here in San Francisco, and you're in that God awful town planning for a wedding that would have been better suited for St. Ignatius and Le Meridien than what you have in mind..."

Rory had had it. "Listen, Lenora. This is the last time I am going to say this. The wedding is being kept in this God-awful town...Oak Harbor, that's its name. The wedding will be kept here, or there won't be a wedding at all," she snapped.

"Well, I never...," the woman drew in a sharp breath. "I told James he was rushing into something that you definitely are not ready or suited for."

Rory had heard enough. "Lenora, I can't do this with you now. I gotta go. Bye." With that, she disconnected the call. She drew in a deep breath and slowly released it as her emotions ran amuck.

She had never felt alone as she did in that instant. It felt like she was fighting a losing battle, and her fiancé, who should have been fighting with her, she wasn't sure what side he was on. The fact that he didn't see anything wrong with the prenup he'd accepted from his parents and even after knowing how she felt about it was very telling. She felt betrayed. How could there be a wedding when they were having so many unresolved issues? She looked down at the phone in her hand, contemplating what to do. After a few minutes, she selected the number she had on speed dial and brought the device back to her ear.

"Hi," James answered on the second ring.

"Hi," she answered softly, wobbly voice.

"Ro, what's wrong?" James asked, alarmed.

A tear slipped down her cheek, and she reached up to wipe it away with her palm. However, her action only seemed to aggravate the issue as more tears came spilling from the dam, running rapidly from her eyes and down her cheeks. Feeling weak, she leaned against the porch's column.

"Ro...say something...please."

She gulped back the sobs that threatened to escape her lips.

"I...I think we should...we should postpone the wedding, James. I don't want to get married like this," she finally said.

There was a long pause. Her tears flowed silently, and her hand tightened around the device against her ear as she waited for him to say something.

James released a defeated breath. "Why are you doing this, Rory? You know I love you...why can't that be enough?" he asked, his voice strained.

A sob finally escaped her lips. "Goodbye, James." Pressing the end button, the phone slipped from her loosened grasp to fall to the floor with a thud. Rory bit her lip to contain her sobs as her shoulders slowly shook, the tears blurring her vision. Just then, there was a flash of lightning followed by the loud rumbling of thunder. The sky just as suddenly burst open, allowing droplets of water to fall to the earth's surface. The rain fell slowly and steadily before it picked up the pace, pelting the porch roof with its amplified fury. It felt like her heart was taking a battering as well, as it squirmed with pain. Rory finally released the heart-wrenching sobs that had been riotously bubbling to the surface.

The holiday was creeping up fast— only three days to go. Rory clicked the checkout button on her Amazon purchases and proceeded to input her credit card information. She'd planned to wait until after Thanksgiving to do her shopping for gifts for the upcoming yuletide season as Black Friday, and Cyber Monday sales were just around the corner, but some of the items she needed to get would be delayed if she waited for the two biggest shopping days of the year. She'd get the other things that wouldn't prove a hassle to receive on time then.

After placing the order, she switched off the laptop and rested on the nightstand. She remained in bed, propped up against the headboard, as she reflected on all the events that had taken place in the past couple of days.

She'd told James that they should call off the wedding, and she hadn't accepted any of his calls since then. She'd gone through the voicemails and texts he'd sent pleading for her to reconsider her decision and him telling her that he would make everything right. She wondered what he'd meant by that. Her heart still ached from everything that had happened, but it also yearned for him, especially in her moments alone when she had nothing or no one to distract her from her thoughts. She'd itched to call him back on several occasions but, at the last minute, had managed to talk herself out of it. She just hoped he wouldn't try to call Andrea. She had chosen to wait until after Thanksgiving to announce her intentions to postpone the wedding as she didn't want that to be the focus of their family gathering to celebrate a year of being together like this after being apart from each other for so long.

"Mhmm, something smells great," Rory quipped as she entered the kitchen to see her mom and aunts flitting around as they prepared food for the barbecue they were planning to have today. Most of the family would be arriving soon to commence their extended family get-together and holiday celebration. The temperature was warmer than usual, so it was perfect for their family gathering. The house would be full of family that she'd grown close to since coming to Oak Harbor and those she hadn't interacted with since Grandpa Sam's funeral.

"Hi, honey. How'd you sleep?" her mother asked, throwing a smile over her shoulders as she used a rolling pin to flatten and stretch the dough she had on the counter.

"I slept well," she answered, wincing inwardly. She'd tossed and turned for most of the night until she'd finally decided to get up and browse the net and get a move on in shopping for gifts.

"Hi, sweetie. Could you take this up to Jules for me? She needs to eat something to take her medication."

"Sure thing, Aunt Cora." Rory accepted the tray of fruit and cereal from her aunt and made her toward her cousin's room on the ground floor, opposite Grandma Becky's. "Jules? It's me, Rory," she called out after knocking. "Your mother gave me your breakfast."

"The door's open," Julia called out.

Rory turned the knob before using her shoulder to prop the door open as she walked through. Julia lay with her back against the headboard, pillows behind her back.

She smiled welcomingly at Rory, but Rory could see the strain behind her eyes. It was evident that even though she'd been on bed rest for the past week that she hadn't been getting much sleep if the dark circles under her eyes were anything to go by.

"How are you feeling?" Rory asked, placing the tray on the bedside table, and staring down at her cousin.

"I've been...better," Julia answered with a small smile.

"Can I?" Rory pointed to the chair beside the bed, indicating she wanted to take a seat.

"Yeah, sure," Jules agreed.

Rory reached for the tray and placed it on Julia's lap before taking a seat and watching her take a few bites of the fruits in the small bowl.

"Have you thought about what I said?"

Julia paused, eating to look over at Rory, her eyes tired and filled with apprehension.

"I did," she replied slowly, nibbling her bottom lip. "I want to try and find my baby's father again but just...not yet. I'll try after I've given birth," she said, her hand coming up to rub her protruding belly.

Rory nodded in understanding. "If there's anything you want to talk about, I want you to know that I'm here for you."

Julia nodded her head and smiled gratefully. "Thanks, Rory. I'm glad to hear that."

Rory returned her smile before rising to her feet. After giving her arm a reassuring squeeze, she left the room. She looked over at her grandmother's door contemplating whether or not she should poke her head inside to greet her. It was still very early. She decided against it, not wanting to disturb her if she was asleep. She just wished she had more time to get to know Becky better, but this cursed illness was robbing her of that. With a heavy sigh, she continued down the hall and made her way back to the kitchen.

"Thanks for taking the food to her, Rory," Cora looked up to say, a smile of gratitude on her lips.

"You're welcome, Aunt Cora," Rory returned with a smile of her own.

"Is she..." Cora hesitated. Her sisters glanced over at her before returning to their individual tasks. "Was she eating?" she finally managed to ask, the angst on her face evident.

"Yes. She ate a few pieces of the fruit, and when I was leaving, she started drinking the cereal," Rory informed her aunt.

The woman sighed, and her shoulders relaxed.

Rory understood Cora's relief. It was evident that the mother-daughter relationship was strained even though it was also clear that her aunt loved her daughter very much. She hoped it would all get sorted before the baby arrived. Although not a mother herself, she knew Jules would need all the love and support she could get in her current state.

The doorbell rang.

"I'll get it," she jumped up before making her way to the foyer. She swung the door open to see Kerry and Dianne standing before her with foil pans in their arms.

"Hi, sweetie," Kerry greeted her.

"Hi, Tessa, Dianne," she greeted back. Dianne smiled in

acknowledgment. "Mom and the others are in the kitchen," she informed them as they stepped inside.

"Okay, thanks," Kerry responded, walking in the direction of the kitchen with Dianne in tow. "Tessa is outside. She's coming with another tray," she called behind her.

"Okay," Rory responded, waiting for her cousin to arrive.

When Tessa finally came up the porch steps, and they greeted each other, they made their way back to the kitchen, where there was a lot of chatter and laughter. Rory smiled at how at ease everyone was with each other.

The doorbell rang again, and she made her way to answer it. This time it was her grand-uncle Luke and his wife Maria as well as their daughter-in-law Sharon and two of her and Charles' three children, Sara and Trevor. Uncle Luke and Aunt Maria went directly to Grandma Becky's room while the others joined those who were already in the kitchen.

Rory found herself as the first responder to every ring of the doorbell, and soon enough, the house was buzzing with quite a number of the Hamilton clan.

The doorbell rang while she sat on the stool, laughing at a joke Kerry had just told as she poked fun at her big sister.

"That's my cue," she piped up, earning chuckles from the others. Rory made her way to the door and quickly swung it open with a broad smile on her lips. Her smile slipped, and her lips slowly formed an *o* as her eyes widened in shock at who stood before her.

"James?"

Chapter Twenty-One

"Hi, Rory."

"What're, how..." Rory felt tongue-tied, her brain befuddled as she stared at the man before her. Her heartbeat erratically against her chest as she stared into the electric blue eyes that stared back at her with hope—eyes she hadn't stared into for nearly a month now.

"I needed to see you," he responded simply, answering the unasked question.

Rory didn't know how to respond to that, and she didn't get the chance to because, just then, she heard, "Oh my gosh, James, you're here. I'm so happy to see you."

"Hi, Mom." James looked over her shoulder, a warm smile on his lips. Rory moved out of the way to allow her mother the opportunity to hug him.

"I didn't know you were coming," Andrea said in a questioning tone the moment they separated.

"It was a surprise," he replied, looking over at Rory before staring back at Andrea.

"Well, I am surprised, and it's obvious Rory hasn't gotten

over it either," Andrea responded, looking over at her daughter before turning her attention back to him. "I'm just happy you chose to come...I may have been longing to see you just as much as my daughter," Andrea confessed.

"I've missed you too, Mom. And I've missed my fiancé very much." At the latter statement, James cut his eyes to Rory, the sincerity of his words palpable from the look he gave her.

"I'm glad to hear that," Andrea replied, pleased. She looked down at his empty hands before casting her eyes outside and then back to his face. "Where are your bags? You are staying for Thanksgiving, right?"

"I am staying," he affirmed with a small chuckle. "My bags are in the car."

"Good," Andrea replied, smacking her palms together and clasping them pleased.

"We can get your bags later. Let me take you to meet the family. There are quite a few that have never met you," she suggested.

"Okay. I'd like that," James beamed.

"Rory, are you coming?" Andrea looked over at her daughter with concern etched into her brows.

Rory managed to steel her expression, giving the woman a small smile. "Yeah, you two go ahead. I'll be there shortly. I just need to use the bathroom really quick," she explained.

"Okay, sweetie," her mother responded. "We're setting up the back patio for the barbecue. Join us out there when you're finished," Andrea instructed.

"Okay," she responded, avoiding James' gaze that was on her. Rory turned and disappeared into the powder room on the bottom floor. She splashed her face with the cold water before staring at her reflection in the mirror above the sink. After a few more splashes, she left the bathroom, ready to smile and pretend that everything was right between her and James.

"Hey, Rory. Are you okay?"

Rory looked over to see her aunt Jo looking at her with concern.

"I'm fine," she replied, plastering a smile on her lips. "What do you guys need help with? What can I do?" she asked, effectively changing the topic.

"We're moving the trays of food out to the patio. You can put it with the others on the table there," Jo instructed.

"Okay," Rory perked up, taking the pan of casserole to go.

Rory spotted James talking with her mother and a few other members of her family a few feet away from the patio. Keeping her head down and her eyes averted, she made it to the stone slab table and deposited the pan. There were a number of foil pans on the table, the mixture of aromas causing her to salivate. Her belly grumbled a little as she remembered she hadn't eaten since yesterday evening.

"Hey...Rory...over here."

She looked over at Dianne beckoning to her. She stood with a few of the cousins Rory hadn't interacted with yet.

Rory made her way over to them.

"Rory, these are our cousins Natalie and Nikki. You already know Aunt Kerry's daughter Sophia and you know Trevor."

"Hi," She greeted everyone with a smile. They returned the gesture.

"So that's your fiancé over there talking with your mom, huh?" Dianne remarked, looking over at her mother and James.

"Yeah," she replied with a smile as she turned to look at James. "That's him.'"

James chose to look in her direction, their gaze connecting one another. James smiled affectionately back at her, but all Rory could manage was an awkward upturn of her own lips. She looked away from him to focus on the conversation with her cousins.

"So, Dianne, is Jake going to make an appearance?"

"I don't know," she replied. "He's been very busy."

"He's been busy a lot lately," Nikki quipped.

"So, Nikki, what do you do?" Rory jumped into the conversation to ask, noting the look of discomfort on Dianne's face. Dianne threw her a look of gratitude.

"I used to work at The Anchor, but I'm currently between jobs, you know."

Rory nodded.

"Plus, I'm planning to move to LA. I'm gonna become an actress. My agent thinks I have what it takes to become a great star," the girl beamed.

"Wow, that's nice. I hope you get your big break," Rory replied.

"Oh, I know I'm gonna get it," Nikki responded confidently.

Rory liked that the girl knew what she wanted and seemed determined to make it happen, but she couldn't help but notice that Nikki was a little arrogant and judgmental of her other cousins. From the moment Rory had joined the conversation, she'd noticed that Nikki tried to find all the flaws her cousins had and sling it in a deprecating manner. Rory didn't like it, and she wondered if the others were as uncomfortable as she felt the more Nikki opened her mouth to speak. If the look Dianne gave her, it meant that she wasn't the only one put off by her attitude.

"Good luck," Rory said simply.

Her attention turned to the back door to see Uncle Luke holding a very frail Becky as she made slow, deliberate steps in the direction of the melee of activities her family was currently involved in. Rory smiled, grateful that her grandmother wouldn't be holed up in her room, missing the activities of the day. She, her mother, and her aunts had tried to coax her to come and enjoy the barbecue to no avail. She was happy that Uncle Luke had been successful where they had failed. Her smile widened when she noticed Julia emerge through the door. She didn't follow them down the steps but had taken a seat on the porch. Nevertheless, she was glad that they had decided to join the celebrations.

Ben, who'd come a short while ago with Marg and his kids, rushed over to help Uncle Luke get Becky settled in one of the wicker chairs. Rory excused herself and made her way over to her grandmother.

"Hey grandma," she greeted smilingly.

Becky looked up at her, her lips turned up in a small smile. "H-Hi Swee-sweet-heart," Becky replied. She tried to lift her hand to Rory's face as Rory knelt before her, but it proved too much for her. Instead, Rory brought her hand to Becky's hand, holding her palm in place and bringing her head forward until her palm curved over her cheek. Becky smiled affectionately at her granddaughter, and Rory did the same. "I'm really glad you chose to join the family," she said softly. Becky slowly brought her head down in acknowledgment.

Noticing Becky's slight shiver and how cold her hand was, she asked, "Are you cold? Let me go get a blanket for you. Even though it's warmer than usual today, I'm sure your still cold." Not waiting for a reply from her grandmother, she headed inside to get the blanket.

Just as she stepped locked the linen closet, blanket in hand, the doorbell chimed. Rory folded the blanket under her arm and went to answer the door.

"Hi, Rory," Trey smiled at her.

"Hey," Rory replied, her brows raising in surprise. "I didn't know you were coming."

"I wasn't planning to," he responded, scratching the back of his neck. "But dad said he couldn't make it because of work and all, you know, and I sorta volunteered to come in his place."

"Great, well, come on in. The party is getting into full gear. I'm happy you came, though," Rory expressed sincerely.

A smile transformed Trey's face at her revelation. "Come on, the party's out back," she inclined in the direction for him to follow her. "Mom's over there. I'm sure she'll be glad to see you. I'm just gonna take this blanket to my grandmother," she informed Trey as they stepped out on the back porch.

She noticed his hesitation.

"You can sit here and keep Jules' company until I'm finished," she offered. "Jules, do you mind?" she asked, turning to her cousin, who seemed to have zoned them out until her name had been called.

"I'm sorry. What were you saying?"

"I was asking if you'd mind it if Trey sat with you for a while," Rory repeated.

"That's okay. I don't mind," Julia accepted.

"Great." She turned to Trey. "I'll be back shortly." With that, she dashed down the three steps and made her way to the patio. "Here, Grandma, I brought you the blanket." Rory bent and secured the warm material around her grandmother.

"Th-Th-Thaaa-nk y-y-you, "Becky responded.

Rory smiled warmly down at the woman.

"Becky, guess what I have here?"

Rory turned to see Maria waving what looked like an album as she came toward them. Becky smiled and slowly shook her head.

"It's an old-school album from back when we were in high school," Maria answered her question. "Boy, I haven't seen these photos in a while," she mused.

"I'll leave you two to it," Rory said. Placing a kiss on her grandmother's cheek, she excused herself.

She grabbed two hotdogs from the tray that her cousins was walking around and serving from, then headed back for the porch. She noticed James staring at her but chose to ignore him. She didn't know what his angle was, and she wasn't quite sure what to say to him just yet.

"Hey, are you coming down?" she called up to Trey, who sat quietly with Julia staring out at the activities taking place.

"Yeah, sure," he replied, rising to his feet. She handed him one of the hotdogs and took a bit of her own, groaning in satisfaction.

Trey did the same. Together they walked over to where her mother, James and a few other members of her family stood talking and laughing.

"Mom, look who's here," she called out, interrupting the conversation.

Andrea turned to them, her eyes widening. "Trey," she said appreciatively. "I'm so happy you could make it." Andrea reached over and gave the young man a warm hug that he returned.

James came to stand beside Rory. "Hey, can we talk?"

"Yeah, sure," Rory replied. After excusing themselves, Rory led him toward the rose garden. That would be a private enough place for them to talk. After a few minutes of walking and admiring the beautiful colors of the flowers that hadn't lost their petals just yet, she stopped and turned to James.

"Why didn't you tell me you were coming?"

James sighed, raking his hand over his face. "I was afraid you'd tell me not to come," he said seriously as he stared at her. "I missed you...I miss you," he emphasized. "Don't you miss me, Ro?"

Rory turned her back from his piercing blue eyes that she was sure could predict just what she was feeling. They'd always had that connection which was why she couldn't understand how he wasn't aware of just how much his actions had hurt her.

"I miss you, James. How could I not?" she asked, folding her arms around her torso to keep herself upright.

She felt warmth on her back but didn't turn around.

"I love you, Rory," James spoke softly, his breath fanning her ear.

She inhaled sharply, the fresh, cold air stinging her lungs.

"I don't want to live without you. You are the best part of my life." Rory swooned as his arms came around her to hug her to his chest and his chin rested at the top of her head. Her eyes fluttered closed. "Tell me you still want a future with me, Ro."

"I do," Aurora's words slipped through her lips. They remained that way for a few minutes, neither saying anything, just taking comfort from being in each other's arms once again.

"How long are you staying?" she finally asked.

"Until Thanksgiving."

Rory's heart fell, and her chest tightened as a wave of disappointment washed over her.

James realized that she had stiffened in his arms and spoke up, "I have to go back to work, Rory."

She stepped out of his embrace and turned to stare into his eyes. Her green eyes, she was sure, reflected how she was feeling at the moment.

"It feels like we're fighting a losing battle, James. Clearly, your priority isn't to get this relationship to work—"

"That's not true, Rory. I'm here because I want to fight for us. I need this to work," James jumped in.

"I don't want to do this. I'm tired."

James sighed, defeated. "Who was that you were talking to back at the barbecue?" he asked.

Rory reared back to look at him as if he had lost his mind. "Are you serious right now?"

He didn't reply but simply stared back at her, waiting for an answer.

"That was my mother's boyfriend's son. In essence, that was my stepbrother-to-be. Also, he's nineteen and in college."

A look of remorse passed over James' face, and he opened his mouth to say something, but Rory beat him to it.

A Spectacular Event

"Let's just get back to the barbecue." With that, she turned and walked back toward the house, not caring if he had followed her.

When they finally made it, her mother came toward them, her face showing concern.

"Mom, what's wrong?" she asked worriedly.

"It's...James," she replied, her eyes darting from Rory to him as he stood a few feet behind her. Andrea dropped a bombshell.

"Your parents are here."

Chapter Twenty-Two

"Did you hear what I said, James? Your parents are here."

"Um...yeah-yeah, I heard...did they say why?"

Andrea shook her head apologetically. "They're in the house, in the family room waiting for you."

"Okay, thanks. I'll Just head inside." James made to move off, but Andrea's next words stopped him in his tracks.

"Rory, aren't you going to go with him to say hi to your in-laws?" she asked, turning to look at her daughter expectantly.

Rory's stomach pitted into tight coils at being spotlighted. "No," she blurted, her voice going up an octave. "I mean, I think James should talk to them first. I'll...I'll greet them after." She felt his eyes on her but refused to look at him.

Andrea looked from Rory to James, her perceptive eyes boring into them. "Okay," she said simply.

"I'm gonna go now," James spoke. He turned and made his way toward the house once more.

Rory watched him retreat back until he slipped through the

back door and was out of sight. She turned her head to see her mother's gaze already on her. Her heart hammered in her chest.

"Why is James really here, Rory...and his parents...is there something else going on that you haven't told me?" Andrea questioned, folding her arms over her chest as she stared at her daughter.

Rory hesitated. "Um, James is here because he took some time off from work to come to see me," she answered. It wasn't entirely the truth, but it was what she was capable of telling her mother right now. As for James' parents... "I don't know why his parents are here, though. I guess I'll find out after he's spoken to them."

"Rory..."

"I'm sure everything is okay, Mom. Don't worry about it," Rory smiled reassuringly.

Andrea stared at her daughter worriedly.

"Relax, Mom." Rory gently squeezed her mother's shoulders. "Everything's fine."

"Okay, honey," Andrea replied, albeit hesitantly. "I'm gonna go see if mom's all right. Let me know if the in-laws...will be staying," Andrea continued, making air quotes over the word in-laws.

As soon as her mother was out of sight, Rory's face fell. Her skin felt like a million tiny pins were prickling her, and her chest felt tight. She was sure that whatever his parents had made the planned trip to Oak Harbor for, it wasn't to apologize to her and tell her that they would support their marriage— that would be a stretch. If anything, she was sure they were probably trying to convince James that he was making the biggest mistake of his life seeking to be attached to her while insulting everything about her mother's hometown.

"Hey, are you okay?"

Rory tried to fix her face before turning, but she failed.

"What's wrong?" Trey asked, leaning his head to stare down at her worriedly.

"James' parents are here."

"Ah," Trey nodded in understanding. "Does your mom know that they're against the wedding?"

"To a point," Rory replied, putting her thumb and index finger together before opening a little space between them. She sighed, her shoulders sagging dejectedly.

"Come on, let's go get some of your uncle's famously grilled steak," Trey said, offering her his arm.

After a few seconds of just looking at him, she hooked her arm with his and allowed him to pull her toward the grill where Uncle Luke stood, flipping steak and burger meat while talking and laughing with his son Charles.

"Sounds like you guys are having a whale of a time over here," Rory commented as they came up to her uncle's side.

"I was just telling this one here some stories about your grandpa back when we were kids. Oh, the trouble we used to get into," Luke looked over at her smilingly.

"I wanna hear," Rory chirped, needing something to take her mind off what was taking place inside the house.

"Your grandfather was a troublemaker through and through, and he always got me to go along with his hair-brained schemes— I never had a choice because he was so goofy at convincing me." Luke chuckled and plated the sizzling slabs of steak for her and Trey. They took a seat on the concrete bench a few feet away from the grill, waiting for him to continue with the story.

"I remember the time the two of us went fishing after our father warned us not to go out that day, but Sam convinced me that it was the best time to do it, and since pops was gonna be out of town, he would be none the wiser. We finally made it to the fishing hole, and guess who was there?"

Rory leaned forward, getting into the story. "Who?" she asked, eager to find out.

Trey laughed at her enthusiasm.

"Rory..."

Rory looked over her shoulder to see James and his parents staring back at her. Her heart rate that she had lessened considerably shot through the roof, and the look on Lenora's face confirmed that all was indeed not well.

She shot to her legs, wishing she had something to hold on to as her legs felt like they wanted to give way.

"Hi, Richard, Lenora. It's so nice to see you." She forced a smile onto her lips as she greeted them with her hand outstretched.

"Hello, Rory," Richard replied, giving her hand a firm shake.

Rory turned to Lenora.

"Aurora," she said simply by way of acknowledgment.

An awkward silence ensued as Rory slowly dropped her hand to her side. James gave her an apologetic look.

"Hi, you must be my beautiful niece's fiancé's parents," Luke walked away from the grill to greet them with a warm smile to lighten the tense atmosphere.

"Um, Uncle Luke, everyone, this is Lenora and Richard," Rory managed to croak out.

Richard shook his hand with a firm nod. When he turned to Lenora, she barely placed her hand in his, offering him a tight smile.

"Could you excuse us?" Rory asked.

Luke and the others nodded okay, and Rory gestured that James, and his parents should follow her back to the house. They followed her.

She noticed the skeptical look her cousin gave her as she passed her and entered the house.

"Exactly what kind of hold do you have over my son?"

Lenora attacked her the minute the door swung shut to the living room.

Rory drew back.

"I'm his fiancé," Rory said in defense.

"Are you?" Lenora shot back, raising an eyebrow in question.

"Lenny—"

"Mom."

Both Richard and James said in warning.

"Why are you here, Lenora?"

"I am here because my son is choosing to forego our family tradition of having Thanksgiving at home with us to come all the way out here to be with you all because you are threatening to call off the wedding."

"I did not threaten your son, Lenora," Rory returned, offended. "James is old enough to make his own decisions, something that you seem to have a problem with so much so that you had to fly all the way here to try and control what he does."

Lenora pulled back as if she had been slapped, eyes wide.

Rory was sick and tired of sugarcoating things to please this woman. It was too much. She needed to speak her piece.

"So, you're blaming me for the problems you've created in your relationship now?"

"Mom, that's enough," James spoke forcefully.

Lenora looked at her son incredulously. "You're reprimanding me after what she's said, after what she's done?"

"What have I done, Lenora? Hmm? Other than loving your son and planning to have a life with him. What have I done?" Rory asked, her voice steely. "You know what, why don't you talk about the fact that you don't like me? You have never liked me because I'm not from your world; I wasn't on your list of potential matches for James. No matter how hard I've tried to fit in, change, or be less of myself to please you, it's never been enough for you. Then you go ahead and give your son a prenup for me to sign because you think that I am with him for his money." Rory looked at the woman disbelievingly as an angry tear ran down her cheek. "I don't need his money; I have my own. As of last week, I'm two million dollars richer."

"I don't care how much money you may or may not have; you are simply not good enough for my son," Lenora sneered.

"LENORA, THAT IS ENOUGH!"

Everyone turned surprised eyes to Richard.

"Rory, I am sorry for my wife. Sometimes she seems to forget that James has a life of his own, and I am apologizing for myself for letting it go on so long."

Rory scrunched her eyebrows in confusion. Not once had she ever heard or experienced Richard come to her defense against all that his wife had said or done to her.

"I realize now and appreciate that you are strong and determined. You've stood up to her in more ways than one, and I want you to know that despite my wife's objections, I am happy that you will be a part of this family. My son needs someone like you."

"Um...Thank you?" Rory gave him a look of unsurety.

Lenora shot daggers at her husband, but he felt her gaze on him. He seemed impervious to her implicit threat and disdain.

"We'll be leaving you guys for now. I'm sure you have a lot to talk about...to work out." Richard looked from her to James, then to his wife.

"Your family is very lovely. I hope you won't mind having us here for Thanksgiving."

"You're more than welcome," Rory assured him.

Richard smiled warmly. "We'll see you on Thursday."

"Okay," Rory said simply.

"Lenny."

Without so much as a backward glance, Lenora stormed out of the room with her husband following.

After they left, Rory turned to James, embracing herself.

"So..." she said simply.

"I'm sorry about mom...she shouldn't have said all those things—"

"I'm actually glad she did," Rory interrupted. "She finally let me know how she feels instead of her disapproving stares and microaggressions. What I don't understand is how you have not been able to see just how much your mother controls your life and how much you make your decisions and adjustments based on what she says. I asked you to rip up that prenup because our love means more than some terms on a piece of paper. We mean more to each other, and that should be enough, but..." Rory paused, looking down at her feet.

James held his breath, waiting on her to continue. Rory looked back up at him.

"Asking you to do that...I watched you struggle with the decision. It was like watching you trying not to disappoint your mother." Rory sighed. "I love you, James...So. Very. Much. But if you can't choose me...if you can't show up for me when I need you, then we shouldn't get married."

A pained expression passed over James' face. "Rory, please don't say that."

She shook her head, resolved. "Let's just get through this Thanksgiving together, and then we can work out the details of...this," she pointed between them.

"What are you saying?"

"We'll talk about it after," she reiterated.

After a few seconds of staring, James nodded.

"I'm headed back out to the barbecue. Are you coming?"

"Yeah. I'll be there in a minute."

Rory left the room and headed for the back porch.

"Rory, sweetie, is everything okay?"

Rory looked up from fiddling with her engagement ring to see her mom staring at her worriedly. Andrea handed her one of the soda cans she held. She reached up to accept it, giving her mother a tight smile.

"I saw James' parents leave a short while ago," Andrea commented, taking a seat in the empty chair beside her.

Rory took a sip of the lemon-flavored drink, staring out at the buzz of activities. After taking in a large gulp of air, she turned to her mother.

"Mom, there's something I need to tell you...It's about me and James...and the wedding."

Chapter Twenty-Three

Andrea groaned, the incessant ringing causing a disrupting sleep. She reached over unseeingly to stop the alarm before burrowing back under the sturdy covers keeping her warm in its safe cocoon. She just needed five more minutes. It was officially Thanksgiving.

Just as she was about to doze off again, her alarm went off. Punching the pillow under her head, she finally opened her eyes, adjusting to the dimly lit room. She reached over to turn off the alarm before sitting up in bed. She used the balls of her hands to try and wipe away the sleep from her eyes.

It was Thanksgiving. She needed to get up and get downstairs. Even though it was still dark out, she was sure her sisters and a few of her cousins had already risen and were in the kitchen prepping for their big day of celebration. Jo and Cora were both gone from her room, given that they were sharing so that the other family members that had chosen to stay over for the night had somewhere to sleep.

Sighing, she finally slid from underneath the covers and

stepped out of bed. After taking a warm shower, she put on some comfy clothes and left the room. She went to knock on Rory's door, but her hand fell away. She knew James was in there with her, and she wanted to give them their space. After what Rory told her about his mother, she had a few choice words that she wanted to tell the witch. She just hoped they would be able to work it out.

Turning away from the door, she headed down the stairs.

"Mmm, it already smells great in here, and I haven't even made my salted caramel-apple slab pie."

"Good morning to you too," Cora smiled, chopping up the seasoning, which Andrea assumed was for the turkey.

"You looked tapped out. We decided not to wake you," Jo confessed with an apologetic smile.

"Well, thank you...I needed that extra half hour, but I'm here now and ready to be put to work.

"Great, you can start by cutting up this bag of pumpkins," Kerry said, holding up the bag for her to see. "I want to start prepping for the pumpkin spice pie."

"No problemo," she said, accepting the bag. "Have any of you checked in on mom?"

"I did," Cora replied. "She's still sleeping."

Andrea nodded in acknowledgement.

"Have you guys heard anything else from the doctor?" Tessa looked over to ask them.

"Not since the last time we took her. We're simply... watching her because she is deteriorating at a rate that is alarming and unhaltable."

Andrea felt the weight of her sister's words like a hammer knocking nails into her heart. It was true that Becky didn't have much time, but it felt more like they were the ones that didn't have time. Come next year, judging by the aggressiveness of her illness that she wouldn't be there.

"I just wished we had more time with her...it felt like we

just got her back, and now we're losing her," Jo said, voicing her own concerns.

"All right, none of that miserable talking...today is a day of giving thanks. Aunt Becky is still here, so let's just appreciate her and everyone that we still have in our lives because at any minute, it can just go like that and leave you wondering if...they knew just how much you...you loved...and appreciated them." Her eyes swam with melancholy.

The sisters and Kerry shared knowing looks. They knew that Tessa was talking about her husband.

"You're right, Tess. We really need to appreciate the ones that are still here," Cora said soothingly.

"Group hug?" Kerry added, her arms already wide open.

The women chuckled as they stopped what they were doing to hug each other.

The women spent the next couple of hours cooking and baking. The others were either lying on the back porch or out running errands. The turkeys were thawed and prepped to be put into the oven.

Andrea's phone rang just as she placed the pie in the oven. Straightening up and dusting her hands on her apron, she fished the phone out of her pocket. Her lips turned up into a bright smile when she saw who was calling.

"Hi, handsome," she hummed.

"Oh, handsome?" he chuckled, the sound reverberating through the receiver and causing her chest to fill with warmth.

"Is it too much?" she asked, resting her back against the counter, the smile never leaving her lips.

She waved off her sisters and cousins, making kissy faces at her. "Are you guys' children?" she mouthed with her hand over the speaker.

"No, I really like it. Coming from my beautiful, talented girlfriend, it's everything."

She swooned.

"What time are you getting here?"

"Why don't you answer the front door?"

Andrea didn't think her lips could go wider but judging by how tight her face felt it had gotten wider.

"Excuse me," she said, walking out of the kitchen and making her way to the front door.

Her heart skipped a beat as she stared happily at the man holding a phone to his ear and a casserole in his hand, his striking blue eyes smiling back at her. "Hi, beautiful."

Her pulse quickened. "I could definitely get used to this." getting on her tippy toes, she puckered her lips to receive Donny's kiss. And just like that, the butterflies teetered over the edge.

"Where's Bruce, Janice, and Trey?" she asked when they separated.

"Bruce and Janice traveled to her parents back in Seattle for Thanksgiving, but Trey will be here a little later."

"Okay, that's nice. Well, I gotta go back to the kitchen to finish preparing the food for later. The men are outback setting up the patio or playing a hand of poker."

"Or I could just stay here...kissing...you." Donny planted a kiss on her lips with each word he said.

Andrea smiled in between the smoothes. "As...tempting...as...that...sounds, I need to get back to the kitchen. We can finish this up later when we've fed the hungry mass."

Donny chuckled, following her into the house. When they made it to the kitchen, Andrea took the casserole and sent him on his way.

"All right now. Everything is ready. Now it's time to go get ready for this shindig," Cora said, shimmying. The others laughed, but as Cora continued shimmying out of the kitchen, they followed suit, mimicking her movements.

"I'm taking a quick shower." Drea announced, then disappeared.

She was relieved to get under the head of the shower, water cascading down her head and running over her body. The time was cold with the autumn breeze that had been blowing, but the kitchen had been considerably warm, especially after spending so many hours in there. Twenty minutes later she was out of the shower, she dried off and donned a pair of blue jeans and a mustard turtle neck sweater before heading back downstairs.

"Ready to get this show on the road?"

She looked over at her sister with a smile and a nod.

"All right then, let's get this show on the road."

Andrea grabbed a few foil pans and stacked them on each other and proceeded to take them out back. The others did the same.

"Yay! Food time!" Sophia, Kerry's daughter, cheered.

Andrea chuckled when the others started to cheer.

"Hey, Mom."

"Hi, sweetie," Andrea smiled at her daughter, who came over to give her a hug over her shoulder.

"James, no greeting for me?" she quipped with a raised brow at her son-in-law.

"Hi, Mom," James smiled, leaning over to give her a kiss on her cheek.

"That's better," she smiled, earning a low chuckle from him.

"I saw Erin and Tracey; I didn't know they were coming."

"Your aunts weren't sure if they would be here either," she replied. "Did you talk to them?"

"Yeah, yeah. It was great catching up with them, plus I think Jules is really happy that her sister is here. She's smiling more— talking."

"That's great to hear, sweetheart," she smiled.

"All right, everyone. Everything's been settled. Now it's time to eat. Here comes the turkey."

A Spectacular Event

Cora came down the porch steps carrying the turkey. There was another loud cheer as the bird was settled in the middle of the two heavy tables joined together.

"Time to eat."

"Hold on, before we go any further, let's say grace," Aunt Maria rose to say.

There were low murmurs of approval before they all joined hands.

Maria prayed. "Father, we thank you for this wonderful meal that has been prepared. Even though we older women were forced out of our yearly tradition of preparing this fine meal, we are thankful for our daughters and nieces who stepped up to present us with this marvelous food and a Thanksgiving to remember. Amen."

A chorus of "Amen" sounded around the table.

Just as they were about to dig into the meal, Lenora and Richard arrived. Andrea looked over at her daughter, noticing that her smile had slipped away, only to be replaced by a look of caution.

"Hello, Lenora, Richard. We're so happy to have you here," Cora rose from her chair to meet them.

"We are happy to be here celebrating with you all," Richard replied with a warm smile.

Andrea tried hard not to roll her eyes. Jo threw her a questioning look.

James' parents took a seat at the table.

"Let's eat. For real this time," Uncle Luke bellowed.

Just like that, trays were being passed, and people were taking their servings of mashed potato, beans, and casserole.

Uncle Luke volunteered to carve the turkey, commenting that it had always alternated between him and Samuel for each Thanksgiving.

"You guys really outdid yourselves," Charles complimented the kitchen team.

Andrea smiled appreciatively at the acknowledgment as the others at the table added their own sentiments. Further down into the meal, Uncle Luke stood again.

"I think it's time to make a toast to what we are all thankful for. I will start and then pass it to you, Becky," he said. "I am thankful to see all of your lovely faces. I am thankful for the time that we get to be together as a family. Nothing makes me happier. I am also thankful for your willingness to play poker with me even though I always beat you."

Many of the table occupants chuckled at his last comment.

Luke lifted his glass to everyone before passing it on to Becky.

She tried to get up from the table, which caused Andrea's anxiety level to shoot up and judging from her sisters' faces, she was sure they felt the same way.

"It's fine. You can sit. I'm sure we'll hear you," Luke said, putting a hand on her arm to keep her from rising. Becky gave him a small smile before turning to the table.

"I-I-I a-aam th-thankful t-t-to beee h-h-here w-with y-you a-all. I a-a-am gr-gr-gra-te-ful f-for this pr-pre-cious t-time. I-It is th-the ooone I ch-choose to cherish th-the m-m-most," she managed to say.

Andrea's heart was heavy, and her chest felt tight. She wanted to rush to her mother to tell her that everything would be okay. She wanted to run away from the table to find a corner to cry her eyes out. But she wouldn't. She needed to stay where she was and be strong for her mother. So, a smile lifted her lips, and she raised her glass like the others to celebrate her mother's words.

Pretty soon, it was her turn. Rising to her feet, she took a look around the table, and her smile brightened. "I am thankful for my family. There is no other way that I can put it. I look at you all, and one word comes to mind...resilience. With everything that has been thrown at us, we have never been stronger. I am thankful for new love, and new additions to our family." Raising her glass to the low cheers of approval.

It was Rory's time to say something. "I am thankful that I get to experience this. Growing up away from all of this, I don't think I truly understood the full meaning of family until now, and I believe it has made me wiser, stronger, and appreciative of holding on to the ones that matter the most." Rory's eyes cut to James, who smiled up at her hopefully.

Andrea looked sharply at the woman across the table who had just snickered. "Is this boring you, Lenora?" she asked, raising a brow.

"Oh, not at all. I think this sharing is quite...cute," Lenora replied with a saccharine smile.

Andrea felt like reaching across the table to strangle the woman. "What you call cute, we call family tradition, where we all actually like being together, not eating gourmet meals and nonsensical cliche talk," Andrea returned with an equally saccharine smile.

With that, the table went quiet for only a moment before everyone resumed their speeches. That was enough out that awful woman. Andrea would make sure of it.

Chapter Twenty-Four

"So, your parents left?"

"Yeah, they're probably on a plane back to San Francisco right now," James replied, drying his hair as a towel hung around his waist.

Rory sat up in her bed staring at him, watching the roped muscles in his forearm undulate with each twist, his back muscles rippling.

"Are you leaving too?"

James' movements stopped, and he turned to face her. Now she had a full view of his broad, tanned chest. She balled her fists together as the itch to touch him overwhelmed her.

"I took another week off from work."

Rory's head hit the headboard, to her sudden surprise. "You took another week? To stay here?" she asked disbelievingly.

James walked over to the bed and bent down before her with his hands clasped together. "I want us to work, Rory. I will do anything you want me to do," he said, eyes pleading.

"You hurt me, James," she spoke softly, her eyes reflective of her words.

"I—" he reached for her hand but drew back. "I know I hurt you, and there is no amount of time that can make up for that but..." This time he took her hand in his. "I plan to spend the rest of my life— the rest of our lives together— making it up to you."

The sincerity in his voice did something to Rory. She gave his hand an encouraging squeeze before she reached over to plant a kiss on his lips. "I want us to work too," she expressed.

A smile lifted his lips. "Does that mean that you've reconsidered calling off the wedding?" he asked with a hopeful look on his face.

"Yes, that's what I'm saying, but...but we still have a lot of work to get to the altar. The wedding is three weeks away, James. I have to know that you will be in this with me 100% whether or not your mother approves."

"Yes. Absolutely," James readily agreed.

A smile perpetuated her lips.

"I want us to spend time with you, getting to rediscover why we fell in love."

"I'd like that." He smiled up at her. "So, since we are rediscovering each other, does that mean I can sleep up here tonight?" he patted the pillow with hope.

"Uh uh. We're not back there yet, buddy."

"So, it's the floor for me then?"

James groaned, eliciting a chuckle from her. Standing from the bed, she went over to her closet to retrieve the comforters for him. Putting on his boxers and a t-shirt, he took the items from her.

"Thanks," he said, giving her a peck before settling comfortably on his makeshift bed.

Rory turned to her own comfortable bed and quickly snuggled under the sheets hiding from the cold night.

"James?"

"Hmm?"

"Are you asleep?"

"No," James chuckled.

"Do you want to snuggle...with me?"

She didn't have to say anything more. He was under the covers bringing her close to his chest under a minute.

A soft smile lifted the corners of her mouth as her eyelids fluttered shut.

The next morning, they showered and dressed together before heading downstairs to breakfast.

"Hi, sweetheart, James. How did you both sleep?" Andrea greeted them as they each planted a kiss on her cheek.

"We slept well, Mom," Rory replied, smiling. "Did everyone leave?"

"Yup, it's just us here," Jo responded.

Rory nodded in understanding. "Hi, Grandma," she turned to greet Becky, bending down and placing a gentle kiss against her cheek.

Becky's lips turned up into a smile, and her eyes brightened in greeting. Rory's heart soared with joy at the lightness she felt in her grandmother. She made a mental note to spend time doing some things to make new memories that she'd have to remember her by.

She and James took their seats at the table. "Where's Jules and Erin?" she asked.

"Jules has an early appointment at the Gynecologist today, and Erin opted to go with her," Cora volunteered.

"Okay, that's great. I know Jules really wanted her sister to be here, so I can imagine she'd want to spend as much time as she can with her."

"She spoke to you about Erin?" Cora asked, surprised.

"Um...not really," Rory tried to deflect. Cora's unwavering, expectant gaze made her cave— a little. "She just said that she missed her and that if she were here, she knew that things would be a whole lot better for her," she confessed.

Cora looked down at her plate of food before looking up at Rory once more. A barely there smile on her lips. "I'm really happy that she has at least one person she's comfortable talking to and having around.

Rory pursed her lips in uncertainty.

"You know how these young adults are...they will choose to let us, the parents, know what is happening with them last, but they're always reminded just how much they need us and that we give the best advice, free of charge.

Rory felt the pang of guilt course through her.

"The important thing is to let her know you love her, Cora." Andrea passed the platter of pancakes to her daughter, then the platter with eggs and sausages, which she helped herself to, passing the platter over to James.

"James, you didn't say when you were going back to Seattle."

"In a week."

"Oh, that's great to hear," Andrea expressed. "I hope you guys get to spend time together."

"We're planning to," Rory responded, giving James a small smile.

"Well, I'm happy for you both," her mother expressed. Rory shared a smile with her.

"Wanna go for a walk?" Rory leaned over to ask.

"I'd like that," he smiled.

After breakfast, they left the house to walk out to the harbor. The air had grown even more chilly, and Rory was sure by the first week of December rolled in, she'd have to draw out her parka.

"Are you cold?"

Rory looked over at James, who stared worriedly back at her. "Just a little, but I'm fine," she promised.

James still shrugged off the coat he wore over his t-shirt and draped it over her shoulders lovingly.

"Aren't you cold now?" she looked up at him with concern in her eyes.

"I'm fine as long as you are."

Rory felt her face heat up, and color whooshed up her neck. When they made it to the harbor, she eagerly allowed him to intertwine their fingers as they strolled along the fringe of the coast.

"This is nice," James commented as they came to a stop and stared out at the endless pool of water pulling and pushing against the pull of the tide.

James walked up behind her to offer added warmth to her back. She shivered but not from the wind blowing around them. His arms came around her waist, hugging her closer to him. He rested his chin on the top of her head. Her hands came up to rest over his in a way that was familiar to them. She missed this. She had been craving it— the ease of being together — no outside interference and influence.

"I missed this," James voiced.

Rory's face settled into a gentle, calming smile. "Me too."

For the next couple of minutes, they stood, her back to his chest, her hands over his resting over her stomach as they stared in comfortable silence at the water and the few birds that were dotting the skyline, probably in search of their prey.

"Rory..."

"Hmm?"

"I love you very much, and I admire your strength and patience for putting up with me these past couple of months when we should have been planning our wedding together."

"I wouldn't say I'm patient. There's been a few times I wanted to knock you upside the head," Rory spoke jokingly to lighten the mood. The words she'd spoken were true, though.

"But you didn't," James joined with a little chuckle. The sound reverberated from him into her, warming her body with its rhythmic cadence. "I have been so oblivious to how my actions have hurt you, and I want you to know that I am working on being better for you because I want better for us. You inspire me, Ro, more than you'll ever know."

Rory lost her breath at the intensity of his words. Even though she couldn't see his face, she was sure if she had been subjected to his electric gaze, she would have melted before him, not that her insides weren't quivering now and her legs didn't feel like jello, but his strong hands were holding her in place.

"I meant it when I said that I will spend every waking moment making it up to you...and I promise..." James turned her in his arms to look seriously into her eyes. "My mother will never come between us again. I won't allow it."

Rory smiled happily at the man she was falling in love with all over again. "I love you...so much," she expressed, lifting up to fit her lips to his. James eagerly accepted her kiss, and before long, he was dipping her to deepen the kiss.

"I want to apologize to you too," Rory said to James as they sat on the wooden deck of the harbor with their bare feet swirling around in the chilling ocean water.

James inclined his head in her direction. "You don't have anything to apologize for, Ro," he asserted.

"I do," she pressed, turning her head to look out at the blue sky. After another few minutes of silence, she finally spoke. "I want to apologize for keeping it from you that I got my inheritance. That was selfish of me." she looked over, giving him an apologetic look.

"You have nothing to apologize for, Ro," James reasserted, reaching over to connect his hand with hers. "You did what you had to do at the time, and I respect you for that."

Rory smiled appreciatively. "I still should have said something. We have to be honest with each other about everything, James, even when it's hard. Even when we argue, that's the only way we can move forward."

James nodded in understanding.

"And...if you think the prenup is a good idea, then I will sign it. I won't fight you on it," she spoke softly.

James straightened up and turned to her. "Ro...I—"

Rory reached over to place a hand against his lip, effectively ending whatever he was going to say. "I trust you, James. I want you to know that if you think this is a good idea, not anyone else, then I will sign it."

James leaned over to peck her lips, a smile on his face. "Did I ever tell you how much I love you?"

"I believe you've said it before, but it doesn't hurt to hear you repeat it so often," she smiled against his lips.

For the next couple of days, Rory and James visited a number of areas of attractions in Oak Harbor. They enjoyed an intimate picnic, a dinner, and a concert over in Skagit. Rory was on cloud nine for the entire visit, so when it came time for him to leave, her mood dampened.

"I'll be back here in two weeks," James hugged Rory and laughed as she pouted.

"But I miss you already," she whined.

He smiled lovingly down at her, his eyes filled with understanding. "I know."

Rory rested her head against his chest, listening to the steady beat of his heart as she prepared herself for their separation.

"Ro, I'm going to miss my flight if I don't get a move on."

Reluctantly she lifted her head and disentangled her arms from around him. James reached for his luggage and placed it in the back of the rental before coming back to him.

Leaning down, he placed a kiss on her lips and caressed her cheek with his thumb.

"I'll miss you," he expressed.

"I'll miss you more," she expressed, mustering a smile.

James turned to enter the vehicle, and Rory stepped away.

She watched the car drive away until it bent the corner and was no longer visible.

Chapter Twenty-Five

"Good morning," Rory greeted her mother with a kiss to the temple.

"Good morning, sweetie," Andrea returned, tenderly reaching her hand to caress her daughter's face against hers. "How'd you sleep?"

Rory separated from her mother and sat in the wicker chair opposite. "Sleep didn't come easy. I miss James," she confessed, staring out at the bay.

"It's only been a few hours since he left," Andrea chuckled.

Rory released a heavy sigh. "I know, but the past couple of days were great; I didn't want them to end," she turned to look at her mother sheepishly.

Andrea's head dipped in understanding. "Pretty soon, you two won't ever have to be apart," she smiled encouragingly.

Rory smiled in return, but the clawing doubt reared its ugly head. Her eyes returned to looking out at the bay's water shimmering under the light golden rays of the early morning sun now fixed in the blue sky. The cold wind blowing across the porch caused her to circle her arms and hug herself for warmth.

"Brrr, it's getting too cold not to have a sweater on at all times," she spoke, shivering lightly for emphasis.

"That's Oak Harbor for you," Andrea responded. "In a couple of days, we won't be able to sit out here without lighting the pit," she tipped her head in the direction of the portable fire pit by the porch railings at the far corner.

"I pray it snows," Rory added hopefully. "It would be in keeping with the vision for a white Christmas wedding," she further expressed.

"Uncle Luke called to say he's bringing a Christmas tree later. So, Cora, Jo, and I thought it would be great if we could all decorate the tree together— to make it an intimate activity that mom can participate in with us girls," Andrea suggested after a period of silence.

"That's a great idea," Rory agreed, turning to her mother with a smile.

"Yeah," Andrea replied with a faint smile.

Rory noted how Andrea's eyes clouded over and the tiny frown at the corner of her mouth. "Mom?" she called out worriedly.

Andrea's eyes blinked into focus, their blue depths settling on her. "I'm sorry, sweetie. What were you saying?"

"I agreed with decorating the tree together, but then you zoned out," Rory explained, observing her mother.

"Oh," Andrea replied, surprised. She rested her hand on her forehead. "I'm sorry. I've been doing that a lot lately," she apologized with a light chuckle before sobering. She turned her gaze away from Rory. "This whole illness with mom has been... upsetting," she finished with a sigh that sagged her shoulders. "That's why this Christmas has to be perfect."

Rory reached over and rested her hand on her mother's arm comfortingly. Andrea turned to look at her. "It will be," Rory promised with a confident smile which Andrea returned.

The two remained on the porch in comfortable silence

until the smell of bacon hit their nostrils, reminding them that it was time for breakfast. Andrea stopped to check on Becky while Rory forged ahead.

"Mhmm, smells like heaven in here," were the first words out of Rory's mouth as she drank in the rich, spicy, sweet scents of cinnamon, nutmeg, seasoned sausages, and bacon bombarding the room.

"Well, that was the reaction I was aiming for. Good morning, dear," Cora threw over her shoulder with a dazzling smile that caused her blue-grey eyes to sparkle.

"Good morning," Rory returned with a smile of her own. "Need any help?" she asked, gesturing to the spread before her. Freshly baked cinnamon rolls, blueberry muffins, and bread rolls were stacked in baskets and flanked by platters of sausages, bacon, and scrambled eggs.

Cora moved from the stove to scoop more scrambled eggs into the low bowl. "You can take down the plates and glasses. Freshly squeezed orange juice is chilling in the fridge," she said, pointing the spatula toward the refrigerator.

Rory nodded, then headed for the cupboards to do as told. Then, a few minutes later, she set the items around the island before removing the juice jug from the refrigerator.

"Good morning, Mom, Rory."

"Good morning." Erin and Jules greeted, walking into the room before taking seats around the island.

"Hi, darlings, hungry?" Cora greeted her daughters warmly, and Rory smiled and waved.

"I'm starved," Erin replied with a sheepish smile.

Andrea came in shortly after that, and everyone finally sat down to eat.

"So, what are your plans for today?" Cora asked, her eyes moving between her daughters as she sipped her orange juice.

"Um, we were thinking about going clamming by Double Bluff Beach," Erin replied.

"Oh," Cora replied, her eyebrows jogging up her forehead. "Are you sure that's safe for the baby?" Cora directed at Jules.

"Nothing's gonna happen to my baby," Jules replied, her lips spread in a grim line.

"I didn't say...." Cora started but stopped at her daughter's stiffened gaze.

"I'll be doing most of the digging. Jules' will just hold the bucket to collect the clams," Erin attempted to ease the tension, which only caused her sister's hardened glare to switch to her.

Rory pursed her lips, unsure what to say to help de-escalate the situation. She looked over at her mother, whose eyes were fixed on her sister, trying to get her attention.

"Uncle Luke's delivering our Christmas tree this afternoon. Can you try to make it back by then? We want to decorate it with mom and maybe take a few photos to remember this," Andrea finally spoke, breaking the silence that had fallen over the table. Her words effectively broke the others out of their thoughts.

"Yes. Of course," Erin replied with an instant smile.

Jules' gaze softened, and her shoulders deflated as she looked away from Cora to offer Andrea a single nod. Rory looked at Cora to see her eyes swimming with anguish and uncertainty.

Erin and Jules left the house after breakfast. Rory opted not to go with them even though Erin invited her. She understood that Jules wanted to spend as much time with Erin as possible before she had to leave. However, Rory didn't know if Erin realized how much Jules looked up to her and craved her confidence. Rory knew the pregnancy was hard on Jules and that she was struggling to decide what to do, especially with what she told her about the father. She only hoped Erin could help her sister make the right decision.

Late in the afternoon, the doorbell rang, and it was Uncle

Luke and his nephew Ben. The piney aroma of the fir tree wafted through the door before they saw it.

"I come bearing a tree," Uncle Luke smiled, corners of his eyes crinkling.

"Afternoon, ladies," Ben smiled.

"Hi, Ben. Were you at the farm with Uncle Luke?" Cora asked.

"No, I wasn't. I was by the Inn visiting Marg, but I saw Uncle Luke's van and the size of the tree. So, I figured I'd help him get it situated for you ladies," he replied.

"Thanks. We appreciate it," Andrea smiled.

After kissing each of his nieces, Uncle Luke and Ben carried the tree to the family room.

"Where do you want it?" he asked, turning to Cora and Andrea.

"Set it up right here," Cora instructed, standing at the space between the French window and the fireplace. So, the men set the tree down where she directed. Then, they stood back to look at it. The tree stood tall, almost brushing the roof, and its beautiful dark green foliage of needles spread out from its center.

Rory smiled appreciatively. She couldn't wait to see it fully decorated and shining from bright lights.

"We could cut the top off, so it fits better," Uncle Luke spoke, pulling Rory out of her thoughts.

All three women looked at the tree and then looked at each other before turning to him to say, "No," simultaneously.

"I think the fact that it's this tall gives it a lot more character," Andrea surmised, and the others nodded.

"All right then, I'll leave you, ladies to giving it more character," Uncle Luke replied with air quotes. "Come on, Ben, let's grab a drink by the restaurant and have a chat," he finished, heading for the door.

"Bye, ladies," Ben saluted with a smile, then turned and followed his uncle.

"Bye Ben, bye Uncle Luke," Cora waved.

"Thanks again," Andrea added as they followed them to the door. She perched by the stairs. "All right, the boxes with the ornaments should be in the attic."

"Where they're always kept," Cora smiled knowingly.

"Let's hope we're right on the money," Andrea chuckled. She sobered shortly after. "It's been so long since we've had a Christmas in this house."

"It has," Cora agreed softly, her gaze going up the stairs. There was a short pause, the air heavy with the unspoken. "We can take the boxes from the attic and put them in the family room. Then, we can start setting it up when Jo and the girls get here. Mom's resting. Hopefully, she'll be strong enough to take this on with us," she suggested.

Rory followed her mother and aunt upstairs and to the end of the hall. She watched as Cora pulled the door latch and a steep ladder unfolded from the ceiling. Then, one by one, they ascended into the spacious room between the roof and the second floor. Rory dodged and swatted the cobwebs covering the space. Light streamed from two large windows on either side of the gabled roof, highlighting the particles of dust swirling in the air and collecting on the wooden floorboards.

"It looks like no one's been up here in years," Andrea said, running her finger along the surface of a mahogany chest before lifting it to her eyes for inspection.

"Drea, look at this." Cora picked up a book from a box and blew the thin film of dust from its cover. Andrea walked over to Cora, and Rory followed.

"Is that..." Andrea's eyes widened with shock as she stared at the booklet in Cora's hand.

"Yeah, it's our Christmas Calendar from thirty years ago," Cora replied, smiling as she flipped the pages.

"That was the year dad had us dress up like Rudolph the Red Nose Reindeer for the twelve days of Christmas countdown," Andrea chuckled. "Remember how mortified I was because I had to wear the outfit to school around my crush?"

"I do. You wouldn't get out of the car. Dad threatened not to buy you the camera you wanted for Christmas before you finally got out," Cora snickered.

"I think he was catching on to me liking someone; that's why he made me wear it," Andrea tapped her chin thoughtfully.

"That would mean Jo and me were punished because of your crush."

"Maybe," Andrea smirked before the two burst out in laughter.

"It was Jo's idea for the outfit. She enjoyed that Christmas more than anyone," Cora smiled softly, and Andrea joined in.

It brought a smile to Rory's lips as she stood back, watching the women talking and laughing, their reminiscing taking them back to happier times. She was glad to see her mother smiling. With all that had been happening to Becky, none of the sisters, it was necessary that they found moments in between to do this and be appreciative of all that they did have. She wished she would have more time with her grandmother too, but she had been preoccupied with the wedding planning, Lenora, and everything else. As a result, she became a prickle of guilt.

"We should show it to mom. Maybe we'll get a laugh out of her," Andrea suggested. Andrea nodded her agreement.

Rory felt a tickle in her nose, and a sneeze followed almost instantaneously.

"That's a sign we need to hurry up and get out of here," Andrea said.

The women went back to their search for the boxes of ornaments. When they found them, they brought them downstairs to the family room. Cora started dinner, and Andrea helped.

Rory opted to sort the decorations. When Erin and Jules came home, they joined her.

* * *

"Yay! Grandma's here," Rory and the others cheered as Jo helped her into the room.

Becky's lips turned into a smile as her eyes surveyed the room. The decorations were strewn over the chairs and the boxes sat on the floor, ready to be hung on the small branches of the tree or draped around it. Jo helped her settle in the recliner close to the tree, and Andrea draped a hand-knitted quilt over her lower half. The fire crackled in the fireplace sending small embers up the chimney.

"Y-You...You've b-b-been busy," she smiled, her face brightened by the orange glow of the fire.

"We just wanted you to have a beautiful Christmas tree, Mom," Andrea replied with a small smile.

"A memorable one," Cora added, caressing her mother's cheek.

Becky smiled appreciatively, and her eyes glistened.

"It a-alreaaady is," she replied, slowly raising her thin hand to rest her palm on top of Cora's. "I have y-y-you all here."

Cora kissed her mother's temple. Then, Andrea and Jo walked over to her and did the same.

"We love you, Mom," Jo said.

Rory placed her palm on her heart at the loving gesture between her grandmother and her daughters. It was an endearing moment where she could tell they were choosing to have this happy moment with her, free from their constant worry.

"Okay, let's get this tree looking like a winner," Andrea slapped her palms together.

Becky, her daughters, and her granddaughters spent the

next two hours decorating the tree. The tree was a sea of colors. Candles, ball ornaments, candy canes, tinsels, and Santa's reindeer hung from every branch. Finally, Cora stood on a stepladder and placed the star on the pinnacle.

"Now it's complete," Erin said.

"Not quite," Cora responded. She took out two small ceramic white doves, their wings spread wide, and brought them up to her mother.

The moment Becky saw them, her eyes watered.

"I know how special these were to you and dad. Even though dad isn't here to participate, I know he would want you to still hang them for you both."

Andrea and Jo came to stand by her.

"I'll help you hang yours, and Andrea and Cora can hang dads," Jo spoke softly. Becky nodded and gave her daughters a watery smile.

"I w-would l-liiike that. I know S-S-Sam w-would t-too," Becky stuttered, her emotions high. Rory and her cousins watched with smiles as they hung the doves in a conspicuous spot on the tree.

"Time for the lights," Andrea spoke, tracking the plug to the socket in the corner. The minute she plugged it in, warm white light twinkled from under the spindly foliage and brightened the ornaments. The star shone brightly from the tree, its golden beams casting hope on the room. The family drew together until they had an arm over each other's shoulders. The tree was indeed a magnificent work of art put together with much effort and love.

Rory looked over at her grandmother, whose face shone with joy. Her mother, aunts, and cousins all wore the same expression. Rory felt her cheeks warm, and a bright smile split her lips.

She wished they could stay like this forever.

Chapter Twenty-Six

"Here you go, ladies. A gin and tonic for you, Cora and Tessa, whiskey sour for you, Andrea, a Moscow Mule for you, Jo and Shelby— last but not least, a martini for you, Kerry." Jake placed the named drinks before their owners and straightened up, dropping the tray by his side. He fixed the towel over his shoulder, a broad welcoming smile on his lips.

"Thank you, Jack," the woman chorused, returning his smile.

"How are Janice and the girls?" Andrea asked.

"They're good. Janice has been a real trouper with this pregnancy, and I love her the more for it."

"When's she due?"

"Late February to early March," he revealed.

"Oh, that's around the same time Jules is due," Cora piped.

"That's your daughter, right?" he asked.

"Yes, that's right," she confirmed.

"That's great too, then. I'm happy for you...Grandma," Jake said, making air quotes.

"Hmph. Don't remind me," Cora groaned with her hand over her face.

Andrea chuckled at her sister's fake outburst of being mortified, as did the others at the table. She knew that Cora was as eager to meet the newest addition to their family.

Jack's eyes cut to the patron, signaling him back to the bar, presumably to be served. "Excuse me, ladies, I'm being summoned, but it was nice catching up with you."

The ladies smiled back at him. "Say hi to Janice for me," Cora requested.

"Will do," Jake replied. "Ladies." He inclined his head before taking off. They watched him until he made it behind the bar to serve the patron.

"You know, I still can't believe that he and Janice got married," Jo commented.

"It does look like an unlikely pairing, but I've seen them, I know them, and they couldn't be a better couple," Shelby spoke up.

"I thought Donny was going to propose," she blurted, gaining the attention of all the occupants at the booth.

"What?" Cora exclaimed.

"Yeah...I know...too soon, right? I mean...I. Really. Freaked. Out, because I'm sure we're not ready to take such a big step. We're still getting to know each other, and as much as I love him, I just don't think we are there yet." Andrea grunted before taking a large gulp of her drink.

"Drea, nothing is wrong with wanting to say yes." Cora reached across the table to give Andrea's forearm a reassuring squeeze.

"Drea, sweetie...listen to me."

Andrea looked over at her cousin.

"Life is short, unexpected, but it's also wonderful and fulfilling when you have the right person to share your ups and downs with." Tessa looked seriously into her eyes. "You love that man, and I can see...we've all seen...how much he loves you," she looked around the table at the other women, waiting for them to agree with her. The others subtly shook their heads in agreement.

"Go with what your heart tells you," she said finally.

"I love you girls," she cooed.

"Aww, we love you too, Drea," Cora returned before they all held hands reassuringly.

"Not that I don't like this nice little kumbaya session we're having here, but why aren't we on the dance floor having fun like we should?" Kerry asked.

"You're right. We came to party. Blow off some steam," Andrea responded. Finishing the last of her drink, she slid out of the booth and stepped up onto the bar's main floor. She allowed the upbeat tempo to move her, her arms going up in the air as she moved her hips side to side.

"You go, girl!" Kerry cheered, getting out of her seat to join her. Pretty soon, the others slipped out of their seats and moved their body rhythmically to the beat as the disco lines bounced off their bodies and the dance floor.

Cheers elicited from the other patrons as they watched them enjoy their time. Pretty soon, the pull of their enthusiasm caused the dance floor to be packed with other bodies seeking to have a good time and it would turn out to be a good night for all.

The following morning Andrea woke up with a bludgeoning headache. Groaning loudly, she rolled out of bed and made her way toward her bathroom for a shower. Hopefully, the water would liven her up, and her headache would recede. But her head remained pounding after the shower. Putting on a comfy sweater and leggings, she made her way downstairs to the kitchen to see what she could take to alleviate the inconvenience.

Putting on the kettle, she removed the honey from the

cupboard and got ginger and a lemon from the refrigerator. After pouring the hot water into a mug, she squeezed the lemon and grated some ginger. She attached a pinch of cinnamon, allowing it to steep. After adding the desired amount of honey, she brought the steaming cup to her lips, inhaling the slightly tangy ginger aroma and clearing her airwaves. She sighed in satisfaction. After a few more sips, she made her way to the family room.

The fresh woody fragrance of the pine wreaths and garlands, intermingled with the sweet holly scent, diffused throughout the house and was indicative of the yuletide season fast approaching. Pretty soon, there would be other scents permeating the air, like the spicy scent of cinnamon and cloves and the refreshing, calming aroma of peppermint. There was already a shift in the atmosphere of the town. Most of the shops had a holiday-themed display. Garland and pepper lights decorated the storefronts, and, in some shops, a beautifully decorated tree was on exhibit, with a few even having a nativity scene set up. The sound of 'Drummer Boy,' 'Silent Night,' and others could be heard everywhere.

"Hi, Mom."

Andrea looked over her shoulder to see Rory standing in the doorway.

"Hi, sweetie," she smiled. "Everything okay?"

"Yeah. It's just I woke up and couldn't go back to sleep," Rory replied, walking further into the family room.

Andrea patted the space beside her on the couch invitingly. Rory came to sit beside her and folded her legs under her, then accepted the end of the throw her mother offered, settling it over her lower half.

"What's that?"

She looked down at the mug in her hand. "Oh. It's just something to calm me. I had a headache," she explained. "I'm feeling much better now."

Rory nodded and gave her a smile of acknowledgment.

"Are you excited about your wedding?"

Her smile broadened. "I am."

Andrea reached over to squeeze her daughter's arm, and Rory reached up to grasp her hand in hers.

"I can't believe that in only a week and a half, I'll be... married," Rory voiced.

Andrea looked over to her daughter and gave her a knowing smile. "I can."

The two sat in comfortable silence, watching the orange embers of flame in the hearth of the fireplace.

"You know...this is becoming my new favorite room in the house."

"Mine too."

***

"Hi."

"Hi."

Andrea greeted back, leaning against the front door as she stared into blue eyes that always caused her to lose her train of thoughts as they stared at each other. "Hi."

"You said that already," Donny chuckled softly, pulling her into his arms and planting a kiss against her temple.

Andrea felt her heart flutter as her cheeks warmed with glee.

"So, you ready to get this show on the road?" he asked.

"Yeah." Kiss. "In about." Kiss. "A minute." Kiss.

Donny chuckled against her lips, his arms tightening around her. "I like the way you think, Miss Hamilton."

"And I...like your response," she smiled back at him.

Donny groaned. "If you keep looking at me like this, we won't make it to the pine tree farm."

"All right. Let's go before I choose to keep you, prisoner, here," she said, patting his chest and moving away.

Donny chuckled again and followed her through the door. For the next couple of hours of driving toward Greenbank, the two talked and laughed, held hands, and shared promising glances.

Andrea loved this, the time they got to spend together. She loved the feeling that she was with someone that just got her. When she was with him, it felt like coming home...sort of how it felt being back in Oak Harbor with her sisters, her mother and having Rory here. It felt like the picture didn't fit together without him in it.

"Are you okay?"

"Mm-hmm," she expressed with a smile.

Donny brought her hand to his lips and kissed her knuckle affectionately.

A few minutes later, they pulled up to the farm. Donny drove through the wide wooden gates down the graveled path lined by fir trees over ten feet tall. A little while after, they parked in the designated parking lot, where there were quite a number of cars already there.

They walked hand in hand toward the small shed-like store to talk to the owners. After signing up, they left in search of the right tree.

"How about this one?"

"Yeah. Sure. That one's fine."

Andrea's hand fell from touching the pine needles of a decent-sized tree to fold them across her chest.

"You're distracted," she pointed out the obvious as he stood with his hands in his pockets, his gaze shifting all over the place.

"Hmm? I'm not," he assured her. Andrea's deadpan look caused him to backpedal. "All right. I admit it. I was a little distracted, but it's because I trust your judgment. I'm not really into all this holiday thing. I would have just put up a few garlands and called it a day. However, being with you makes me want to do these things."

Andrea wrapped her arms around his waist as she smiled up at him. "I'm glad, but it feels like there is something else here."

Donny smiled hesitantly as he untangled himself from her. "You're right. There's something I need to tell you...ask you, actually."

Her heart skipped a beat, accelerating as her eyes widened when Donny reached into his pocket and came up with a jewelry box— a ring box.

"Donny, what're you..."

"I love you, Drea...more than I think you know..."

Her heart slammed against her chest, and her mouth felt dry.

"I think we are moving in the right direction, and so I think the best thing to do to move our relationship forward is to ask you to m—"

"Donny, don't."

"—move in with me?"

Andrea's brows furrowed in confusion. "What?"

Donny opened the box to reveal a single key on a Whidbey Island key chain.

"I'm not saying you have to come live with me, just that it would be nice to have you think of my home as your home too, not that you don't have your own house, and I would never dream of taking you away from your sisters and your mother. I just want you to know that you're welcome to come and go as you please and—"

Andrea placed a finger against his lips, halting his word vomit. "Thank you. I love it," she said with a smile before raising up to touch her lips to his.

Donny released a relieved chuckle. "This went better than I expected."

Andrea smiled, then turned back to the tree she had been observing. She felt Donny's hands circle around her shoulder, bringing her back close to his chest. "I love you," he breathed against her ear.

Andrea smiled and lifted her hand to rub his. Her smile fell when she realized that she was disappointed that Donny hadn't been planning to propose.

After choosing the tree, she followed him to his house and helped him set up and decorate the tree before heading home.

Andrea sighed, resting her back against the door. How could she have felt so shattered when Donny opened the box to not see a ring? She didn't want to think about why she had been so disappointed. Shaking her head, she pushed away from the door and went for the stairs.

Just as she stepped on the first rung, a noise coming from down the hall caught her attention. She moved away from the stair and went to investigate.

"Mom? What are you doing?"

Andrea stared at her mother in alarm. Becky slowly turned her head to look at her daughter, who was staring at the walker. She gripped it with her hands, then back to her face.

"Let me, let me help you." Andrea sprang into action, making her way to her mother. Becky shook her head no and stopped her in her tracks. She watched her mother turn and then used her strength to roll the walker forward. She itched to go over to her.

Becky slowly continued to roll herself forward, but on her fourth step, she stumbled, almost falling and the walker going out from under her.

"Mom," Andrea spoke up in alarm, rushing to her.

"I'm fiiine," her mother affirmed, continuing to roll herself forward as if nothing had happened before.

A Spectacular Event

Andrea watched helplessly as her mother rolled herself to the back door and disappeared through it. After a few minutes of just staring at the door, she finally decided to go through it.

She found her mother sitting in one of the wicker chairs, staring out at the water. She took a seat across from her and stared out at the water.

"I kn-kn-knoow y-you're sca-scared. I-I a-am sc-scare-d t-too, but I a-am h-happy to h-have you a-all here with me. Th-That is en-enough for m-me." Becky looked over at her daughter, her brown eyes reflecting her love. "I l-love y-y-you g-g-girls. Always. J-Just be h-ha-happy."

Andrea reached over to grasp her mother's frail hand in hers. "I love you, Mom," she expressed. Her mother was dying, but she had accepted that. It was time for her and her sisters to acknowledge it.

Chapter Twenty-Seven

"Shianne! Carly! Over here!" Rory waved excitedly at the two women disembarking the ferry.

They both looked up and waved vigorously, their faces breaking into bright smiles. As soon as they were standing on the dock, they quickly made their way toward Rory, their carry-ons in tow.

The three women crashed into each other as their arms came up for a group hug. They laughed uncontrollably. Rory used the back of her hand to wipe at the tears that settled at the corners of her eyes and tried to calm down.

"You guys don't know how happy I am to see you both," she expressed.

"Trust me. I don't think you're as happy as I am. A whole year of teaching in Japan and being away from my best friend and everything familiar has taught me to appreciate all the memories we've made so far and the ones we're going to make," Shianne commented.

Rory smiled knowingly at her best friend.

"I just wish I'd been here to help you with all these plans

and maybe sock that mother-in-law of yours. I can't believe it's only four days until the wedding," Shianne continued to say.

Rory chuckled. "I know," said with feeling, staring appreciatively at the woman. She knew that Shianne would do anything for her, but it wouldn't have been fair to have her leave her job in Japan to help her fight this battle.

"I'm just really glad you're here now," she said, her eyes filling with reassurance as she smiled at her. She turned to Carly. "Both of you."

"We're happy to be here, too," Carly smiled back.

The three women turned and walked down the wooden deck toward where Rory had parked.

"All right, I wanna hear all that you've been up to these past couple of months. Full detail," Shianne instructed, calling shotgun.

Rory started the ignition before looking over at her best friend. "I almost called off the wedding."

Shianne's eyes widened as she, in surprise, "What?"

Rory chuckled. "It's a long story."

"I bet it is," Shianne returned, earning a snicker from Carly in the back seat.

"And we only have a thirty-minute drive back of Oak Harbor," Rory revealed.

"Well then, you better get a move on with this story then," her friend replied, staring at her expectantly.

Rory shook her head, a grin pasted on her lips. She pulled out of the parking lot before relaying all that she hadn't told her friend on their usual weekly call check-ins.

"You have kept far too much from me, Rory. I could just wring that woman's neck for hurting you the way she did," Shianne shook her head in anger. "James is lucky you love him because I'm tempted to do the same thing to him," she seethed.

Rory reached over the console to hold her friend's tensed hand, squeezing it reassuringly.

In true form, they made it to the property within thirty minutes, and her friends marveled and complimented on the inn's beauty, now decorated for the Christmas season.

"This is where we're staying?" Shianne asked, twirling around the large lobby while Carly stood still staring at the grand double staircase decorated with garland running up the railings, with gold balls and red ribbons breaking up the green uniformity while small lights blinked at intervals. Rory could tell she was in awe too. She wondered how they'd react to the sitting area in the back that had an almost floor-to-ceiling Christmas tree, beautifully decorated by her and Marg.

"I would spend a month here if I didn't have to go back to Japan to those little rug rats," Shianne said before a sour expression crossed her face. "Make that two months."

Rory grinned knowingly. Just then, she spotted Marg coming from the kitchenette.

"Hi, Marg, these are my friends Shianne and Carly," she informed her.

"Hi, it's nice to meet you both," Marg responded with a smile. "You're the maid of honor and one of the bridesmaids, correct?"

"Yes."

After exchanging a few more pleasantries, Rory assured Marg she would show her friends to their rooms. The inn had been booked for the rest of the holiday period up to the day after New Year to house her friends and family who would be staying there.

"So, you're going back to teaching after the honeymoon?" Shianne asked as they strolled across the lawn toward the gazebo at the back of the inn.

"I don't know," Rory confessed. "My grandma is very sick, and she only has a couple more months left. I was thinking about staying here a bit longer."

"Have you talked to James about staying?" Carly asked.

Rory released a burdened sigh as she crossed the floor of the gazebo to sit down on the sectional in the corner. Her friends came to join her.

"With everything that's happened. I don't know. Everything still feels...fragile."

Her friends nodded in understanding.

"So...this is where the wedding will be held, huh? Shianne asked, looking around the gazebo, her eyes unreadable.

"Yeah," Rory confirmed. "Jenny's team is coming to transform this place into a magical winter wonderland the day after tomorrow."

"Not bad. I like the view of the harbor and those mountains in the distance. It's already beautiful," Shianne smiled.

"It's a magical place," Carly chimed in.

Rory smiled happily. "I'm so glad you guys are here," she restated, and she really was.

"There is nowhere else that I'd want to be," Shianne returned.

"All right, time to meet the rest of the family." Rory rose to her feet, prompting the others to do the same.

After introducing her friends to the family, she made her way upstairs, leaving them to catch up with her mother.

Rory could hear James' voice coming through the door as he talked on the phone. When he'd come back over a week ago, she had been over the moon, but then his phone rang, and he had to take it. He had spent hours on the phone getting the junior associate to take over the case until he got back up to speed. She understood the implications of him passing off the case to be here, and she was happy that he was showing her his commitment, but she wouldn't lie that it didn't bother her that he'd been on the phone since she left to pick up the girls over two hours ago and here he was still on the wretched device.

She turned the lock and pushed the door open.

"Hi, babe," Rory greeted with a broad smile, holding up the pastry bag she got at Kerry's bakery.

"I got you something."

"We'll finish this later. I gotta go," James spoke into the phone before ending the call. Walking over to her, he took the bag with one hand while using the other hand to hold her chin and tip her face upward to receive the kiss he planted on her lips.

"Beignets?" he asked when their lips separated.

Rory nodded.

"Mmmm. I can't wait to bite into this," James hummed in delight.

Rory smiled at his enthusiasm.

"Did you happen to see Ethan when you were at your cousin's?" he asked after taking a sizeable bite of the airy fried dough doused in powdered sugar.

"No. Why?"

He took his time chewing the pastry before swallowing. Rory watched him, waiting for his answer.

"We were talking about his career switch from a corporate lawyer to an environmental one. It's just amazing how easy it was for him to make that choice," he finally responded.

"Yeah, it is, but I guess he finally found his calling plus, it doesn't hurt that Aunt Kerry lives here and is also passionate about the environment, so..."

"Hmm."

"So...when do your parents get here?" she asked, keeping her tone even and as casual as she could manage.

"Dad called earlier to say they'll be here tomorrow, and the rest of the family and friends they've invited will arrive the day after," James responded, watching her. They've already booked rooms at the hotel back in town.

She managed to muster a small smile. "That's great. I'm glad they'll be here for you."

"For both of us, Rory," he jumped in to say, closing the distance between them and pulling her into his arms. "They'll be here for the both of us?"

She looked up at him with a raised brow. "Dad'll be here for the both of us," he amended.

Satisfied with his comment, Rory rested her head against his chest, listening to the rhythmic beat of his heart that did something to calm her.

"I don't think your mom will ever like me," she breathed out softly.

"That's her loss," he replied.

After the two separated, they made their way downstairs to greet her friends. His best man and groomsmen would be arriving tomorrow and staying at the inn.

"Well, look who the cat dragged in? I gotta say you're looking more decent than usual since my best friend decided to make an honest man out of you."

"Ha ha, very funny, Shianne. I see that a year in Japan hasn't improved your manners," he retorted.

After a tense few seconds of the two of them staring down at each other, they burst into laughter. James hugged Shianne.

"Glad you're back."

"Glad to be back."

James turned to Carly. "Carly," he greeted with a broad smile.

"Hi, James," Carly greeted, accepting his hug.

* * *

Rory sat by James at the rehearsal dinner, fidgeting with the straps of her lilac-colored dress as the rest of their wedding party stared at them with varying expressions. The one that stood out to her the most was the scowl on Lenora's face and how often she'd caught her staring at her, her brilliant blue eyes filled with rage.

Instead of focusing on how great a job Jenny had transformed Willberry Eats into a sophisticated setting decorated with pepper lights, garlands, and wreaths, not to mention the perfectly set long dining tables that they'd swapped out the regular tables and chairs for. Even though it hadn't snowed as forecasted, the windows had been frosted to give the appearance that it was. No, she hadn't been able to take the time to admire and appreciate it all because of her mother-in-law's obvious displeasure.

For the third time that evening, she wondered if she was making a mistake. She felt the warmth of James' hand on her thigh, which prompted her to look up at him.

"Are you okay?" he mouthed, as his eyes full of concern stared at her.

Rory swallowed down the lump and forced a smile on her lips as she nodded 'yes.'

James was not convinced, but just as he went to make a comment, the sound of a utensil clinking against a wine glass caught their attention. Uncle Luke was on his feet, glass in hand and a bright smile on his lips.

"I would like to propose a toast to my grand-niece, Rory and to her loving fiancé James," he started. Rory felt her cheeks already starting to warm over.

"I know your grandfather would have been happy to be here to witness this, but I also know he is smiling down on you right now. He would want you to know how proud he is of your accomplishments and for always standing up for what you know is right. I believe that you are both good for each other, and I know your union will be a great one.... To Rory and James," he finished with his wine glass raised in a toast. The others raised their own glasses in acknowledgment.

"This is ludicrous. Really? Who doesn't know the difference between a salad fork and a shrimp fork?"

Rory's heart sank to the bottom of her chest.

"Lenny," Richard turned to say through clenched teeth.

The woman looked at her husband before looking away, the scowl a seemingly permanent setting on her face.

Brody, James' best man, was the next person to get up with glass in hand.

"I said I was going to leave all the embarrassing stories of James for the actual wedding reception, but how could I resist?"

"Brody," James hissed in warning, but this only encouraged him to continue to the delight of his audience.

"When we were in college for our initiation into our Sorority, we were dared to..." Brody looked over at James, smirking. James' eyes, in turn, shot daggers at him. "Well, I'll leave that story for another time. Congratulations to both of you!" Brody finished, holding his glass in the air.

Many people got up to wish them well or to tell old embarrassing stories about them. But they were enjoying it. Rory loved hearing the stories about James, as did he about her. They sat teasing each other. Everything was going well until...

"I would like to say a few words."

Silence fell over the party as every eye turned to Lenora.

Chapter Twenty-Eight

Rory's heart thrummed wildly against her chest, and the air jetted through her lips in rapid succession as she watched her mother-in-law stand from her seat, indicating that she wanted to say something. Somehow, she knew that whatever the woman had to say would not be good, and the impending anxiety attack was clawing itself to the surface as she waited.

Lenora lifted her champagne flute, holding it with both hands close to her chest. "Firstly, I want to say that James, my son..." she turned her attention to James, who sat stiffly beside Rory as if sensing that his mother was up to something troubling.

"I love you very much, and I want you to be happy, believe me, I do." The woman took in a deep breath and looked around the room of expectant faces before continuing. "With that being said, ever since the day you were born, I knew you were special and that whatever you did, your father and I would have been proud of you. You have been responsible, caring, and someone who sees the good and usefulness of everyone even when at times it is so far from the truth." Her eyes cut to Rory before settling back on her son.

Rory's heart clunked to the bottom of her stomach.

"You've always had a soft spot for the less...fortunate. It was like you saw it as your purpose, your chance to make a difference. I want you to know that I will stand by your side, even when I can see that you're making a mistake taking on projects that aren't yours to transform because I will always be here for you, through thick and thin." Lenora extended the glass in the direction of James and Rory as she finished. "Congratulations to you both, and good luck."

After Lenora took her seat, the room remained silent as the audience had been stunned into silence. A few people threw furtive glances at the two people the dinner had been in honor of.

Rory felt like she was going to be ill. She felt like nothing. That's how Lenora had described her, and her blatant refusal to acknowledge her by name in her speech proved she would never see the need to treat her any differently.

"Rory..." James spoke softly from beside her.

"I need to get out of here," were the first words out of her own mouth.

"What? Now?" James asked, surprised. "Rory, just let me—"

But she wasn't listening.

The chair scraped against the tiled floor as she pushed it back and shot to her feet. Her family and friends stared at her in concern. Andrea rose to her feet, staring at her daughter in apprehension.

"Rory," James said helplessly, reaching for her hand, but she subtly shrugged off his hand, held her head straight and walked out of the restaurant.

As soon as the cold winter air rushed across her face, the bitter reality hit her— she couldn't get married to James, not in this current state. A guttural sob escaped her lips as she sagged against the restaurant, her knees on the brink of buckling beneath her.

She heard the soft jostle of the door opening, but she was too pained to care who had just stepped through. A pair of hands lifted her under her arms until she was leaning against them as they hugged her tightly. This time Rory sobbed louder, the tears clamoring over each other as they flowed rapidly down her cheeks and dripped from her chin.

"I-I c-can't believe sh-she d-d-did that," Rory stuttered through her tears.

"I can. It's because she's a real witch, a pointy ear, green face filled with pimples and long talons for fingernails witch," Shianne spat matter-of-factly. This earned a chuckle from Rory.

As the two separated, Shianne reached up to wipe the tears from her face with the napkin she'd brought.

"Where's my mother?" she asked, trying to get a glimpse of what was going on inside.

"She's talking-arguing with the monster-in-law."

Rory sighed. "That's what I was afraid of."

"Hey, don't think about that now. How do you feel?" Shianne asked, looking into her eyes.

"Ro."

She looked behind Shianne to see James standing there, eyes tired and a look of desperation on his face.

"I'll give you two some privacy." Shianne moved away from Rory and stepped back inside.

"I had no idea Mom was going to do that," he spoke, his voice shaky.

Rory inclined her head in agreement as she stared out at the darkness.

"Ro. Look at me...please."

Taking in a deep breath to steel herself against the numbing cold and whatever he had to say, she spoke, "The wedding is off, James."

"No, don't say that. Ro. I love you. My mom doesn't factor into this. What she said in there was because she realized that she lost."

"That's just it, James," she stopped him with a shake of her head before looking him squarely in the eyes. The dim lamp lights reflected against his translucent blue irises, now glistening with unshed tears of his own.

"I am not in competition with Lenora— it should have never gotten to that point. All I wanted was for her to like me and not be in a constant fight with her about who knows you better or whose opinion matters most to you. I am tired, James. I don't want to do this anymore— I can't do this for the rest of our marriage."

"I know," James readily replied. He ran his fingers through his hair frantically. "Please, Rory...just let me talk to her. I can't lose you."

"I'm sorry, James. I...I can't." She turned and made her way down the path ignoring James calling after her.

Ten minutes later, she'd made it to the house. After collecting her key off the hook, she drove away from everything. She needed to be alone.

Fifteen minutes later, she found herself down by the marina, which had gradually become one of her favorite spots.

Rory strolled down the festively decorated boardwalk, admiring the way the lights illuminated the water, the buildings closest casting their reflection in the pristine mirror of the marina. She firmly pulled her parka together and zipped it together from the chilly gale that seemed to be picking up in speed and intensity. In a way, she guessed it was a reflection of how she was feeling at the moment— alone and afraid. She didn't know how to move on from this. She didn't even want to think about it.

A tear slipped down her cold cheek as she observed the couple walking ahead of her. They were walking hand in hand and leaning into each other as they whispered in each other's ears and giggled. Deciding it was too much, she stopped and made her way over to one of the benches facing out. The coldness of the metal seeped through the soft material of her dress and into her legs. She wished she'd stopped to put on some pants or at least some jeggings.

Her mind flashed back to James and the pained expression on his face when she walked away from him. It had broken her heart to have to hurt him like that, but it couldn't have been helped. She'd wanted him for so long to stand up to his mother for her, and instead, he had tried to rationalize her actions. Maybe Lenora had been right. Maybe he only wanted her because she'd proven to be a challenge— one that he believed he could save in some way.

A soft sigh left her lips.

"Hey."

She looked up to see James staring down at her, eyes filled with caution.

Rory furrowed her brows, surprised by his presence.

"Trey told me I might find you here," he answered her unspoken question. She remained silent, staring up at him. "Can I?" he asked, pointing to the empty space on the bench.

Rory moved over to allow him more space. The two sat for a while staring out at the water, neither saying anything. Rory threw furtive glances at him before turning her attention back to the water.

"I told mom that she's not welcome to our wedding."

Her mind ran a mile a minute at his surprising revelation.

"I told her that if she can't accept that you are the only woman for me and that I can't live without you, then she is prepared to no longer have a son in her life."

"James," was all she could manage to say as she turned fully to stare at him.

James turned to her with a small smile. He reached for her hand, and she let him. "I love you, Rory. I won't ever stop saying it because it is the truth, and I am sorry I didn't do it sooner but as much as I appreciate my mother for all she and my dad has done for me, you are my future now, and it hurts me when you're hurt. I want you to know that it doesn't matter who tries to hurt you. I will always stand up for you. I will always defend you because that's what love is."

Rory was overwhelmed. Her heart was filled with joy. Reaching up, she cupped his cheek lovingly. James placed his hand over hers and squeezed her fingers softly.

"There's something else."

"Oh really?" she asked with a soft chuckle.

James released a hearty chuckle of his own and took an envelope from the inside of his jacket.

Rory stared from the envelope to him with questioning eyes until he removed the papers. Her eyes widened.

"I had this with me the last time I was here, and I was going to do to it what I am about to do now."

"James, what're you..." she started, staring in alarm at the paper he'd started ripping.

"I don't want there to be anything but trust between us, Ro. I don't need a prenup because I know that our love is strong enough to withstand anything that will be thrown at us. I will spend all of my life making sure you know just how much I love and appreciate you."

Her heart was a pattering mess. "I love you," she breathed, then a broad smile transformed her face.

"I have one more surprise. Ethan offered for me to join him at his new environmental law firm. I'm thinking about making an investment in it."

"James, that's too much. I don't want you to give up everything just to please me. You have a life back in San Fran...our home is there."

James cupped her face in his hands and planted his lips against hers. When their lips separated, he looked lovingly into her eyes. "You're my home," he affirmed.

Rory smiled.

"I can see that you love it here, and it's starting to grow on me too. I know that you also want to be with your grandmother now that she doesn't have much time. Family is important, and I don't want to take you away from yours, seeing that you're just building a relationship with them after all these years."

"But what about my teaching job back in San Fran?"

"You can apply for one here, or I don't know, maybe you can spend time focusing on your art," he suggested.

"What about your mom?" Rory asked softly.

"What about my mom?" he asked, furrowing his brows.

Rory gave him a deadpan look.

James released a sigh of frustration. "Ro, it doesn't matter what anyone thinks— not my mother, not yours or anyone else. As long as we're happy."

Rory nodded her head. "You're right," she acquitted.

"Then say it with me," he instructed.

"No—"

"No..."

"One else matters."

Rory reached over to plant an endearing kiss against his lips. "I love you," she repeated.

"I can't wait to start the rest of our lives together," he breathed out.

She reached over to join their lips together once more. She jumped back in surprise when a single snowflake landed on her cheek before sliding down, leaving a trail of moisture as it slipped to the ground. She and James looked up simultaneously as dozens of snowflakes fluttered down toward them.

Epilogue

"Sit still, Rory. You're too jittery."

How could she not be? She was getting to marry the man of her dreams. Knowing that James would be waiting at the altar for her filled her stomach with knots but the good kind. While her bridesmaids fussed around her, she was lost in her own world.

"Rory?"

Rory looked into the mirror to see her mother standing behind her, wearing a bright watery smile. Indicating to the makeup artist that she needed a minute, she got up from the chaise.

Andrea's hands covered her mouth as she stared proudly at her daughter.

"You look...beautiful," she expressed in awe.

Her heart swelled, and a bright smile broke out on her lips at her mother's appreciation. "You sure it's not just the dress?" she asked jokingly, holding it up at the sides.

"I'm sure," Andrea replied seriously. Walking over to her, she placed a hand against her cheek. "It doesn't matter what you wear, Rory. You will always be beautiful to me, inside and out."

Tears pooled in the corners of Rory's eyes. "I love you, Mom...so much," she spoke with feeling.

Andrea squeezed her cheek lovingly. "I brought something for you," she said, bringing out a jewelry box. "Your something old."

Rory reached for the box and carefully flipped the lid open. A gasp of surprise and wonder escaped her lips. "Mom, it's beautiful," she said, looking from the string of pearls to her mother.

"It was mom's. She got it from her mother, who got it from her mother," Andrea revealed. She reached for the pearls, and Rory turned her back, allowing her to secure it around her neck.

The two women stared at their reflections in the mirror, their eyes pooling with unshed, happy tears.

"Perfect," Andrea breathed out. Rory wasn't sure if it was the jewelry dangling from her neck or her that her mother was referring to, but, at that moment, it made her feel special and important. She reached up to rub the hand holding her shoulder in a loving manner.

"I'm gonna go so that you and your ladies in waiting can finish getting ready. Plus, I wouldn't want Jenny to scold me for making you cry and messing up your makeup. We wouldn't want to get off schedule now, would we?"

Rory giggled at her mother's comments. "She's already reminded me that the heaters can't go past a certain time, so we have to get the show on the road as scheduled, no excuses."

"I'll see you out there." Andrea placed a kiss against her daughter's temple and slipped out of the room.

"Oh pretty, pretty," Shianne gushed as she touched the pearls against Rory's neck. "You already have something new, something borrowed and something old. How about something blue?" she asked, opening her hand to reveal a blue garter. Rory laughed and reached for the piece of material.

"It's far from traditional, but I like it," she thanked her best friend.

"All right, everyone. It's almost time. Please tell me you're all on the last of your preparations." Jenny stormed into the room like a force of nature, an earpiece with a microphone attached to one side of her face.

"Rory, you look lovely, darling. Are we ready to get this show on the road?"

Rory had to bite her lip to prevent the unseemly sound that threatened to escape them. She looked around the room to see that her friends had the same looks.

"Just my makeup needs some retouching," she answered.

"All right, that's good." She subtly signaled for the makeup artist to come and finish up. "We start in the next fifteen minutes, ladies. Please ensure our bride walks down the aisle on time." With that, she left the room, probably to check on other things wedding related.

"You heard the headmistress, ladies. Let's get cracking," Shianne spoke in stunned silence.

At this, everyone broke out in laughter.

True to her words, in fifteen minutes time, her bridesmaids left the room to go meet the groomsmen they would be marching with. Rory could hear the soft flowery music as it floated from the outside up to the room they were using on the second floor of the Inn.

She made her way down the steps, Shianne holding the train to prevent her from tripping over the material.

"Ready?" she asked, staring into her friend's eyes.

A smile broke on Rory's lips. "I'm ready." Her smile slipped a bit when she noticed the woman behind Shianne. Her maid of honor turned her head, her own smile slipping.

"Want me to kick her out?" she asked seriously.

"No. It's okay," Rory assured her. She turned to the woman and gestured for her to follow her to the small kitchenette. As soon as the door closed behind them, Rory whirled on her. "If you're here to threaten or insult me, just know that it won't work, not this time," she warned.

Lenora put her hands up. "That is not my intention," she spoke softly.

Rory folded her hands over her chest as she waited for the woman to continue.

"I know my words might not mean much to you now, but I do want you to know that I am sorry...for everything. I shouldn't have treated you the way I did. That was...wrong. Disgraceful."

Rory didn't know what to make of this, but she remained quiet as she waited for the woman to finish.

"I love my son, Aurora, very much, and I think that love made me hold on a little too tight. It wasn't my place to dictate who he should love, and for that reason, I have lost him." A tear slipped down her cheek.

Rory felt her anger slip a little. She understood where the woman was coming from, and she knew the devastation of not having one parent in her life. She didn't want that for James.

"He loves you very much, and I know that you love him too. Please take good care of him, Rory."

Rory's head went back in shock. That was the first time the woman had called her by Rory.

Lenora turned and walked to the door.

"Lenora, wait."

She turned to look at Rory, who came to stand before her.

"I am not okay with what you did or the way you treated me. I am far from it."

"I know, and I am sorry for that," the woman jumped in to apologize.

"But it's also not my intention to take James away from you. You're his mother. Nothing can replace that bond."

"What are you saying?"

Rory looked into the woman's blue eyes, so reflective of her son's. "What I am saying is, you're welcome to come to the wedding and to visit us in small doses for now. Ultimately, it is James' decision to accept you back in his life but just know I won't be in the way."

The woman's face brightened, and a smile of gratitude graced her lips. "Thank you, Rory," she said, reaching over to give her hand a warm squeeze. "You really are a good addition to this family," she voiced before turning and leaving the room.

Rory stood in the kitchen going over what had just transpired between her and Lenora. She was still wary, but something deep down told her that she could trust the woman's words. She would do that. It didn't mean they would become buddies, though. Lenora, in small doses, was enough for her.

Rory, it's time," Shianne burst through the door to inform her. "Please tell me you haven't changed your mind again."

Rory laughed at her friend's obvious distress. "Shianne, relax. There is nothing in this world that could prevent me from walking down that aisle today," she assured her.

"Good. Now let's get this show on the road," Shianne beamed.

The soft music floated through the open door, indicating that it was time for the procession to begin.

Rory watched as each of her bridesmaids walked through the door on their way to meet the groomsmen that would escort them down the aisle. She couldn't wait for her turn. Her heart felt like it would burst.

Shianne turned to her. "This is your day, sweetie, only you and, by association, a little bit about James." The two laughed at the latter part of her statement. "Just be happy." Shianne touched her cheek affectionately before turning and making her way outside. A few minutes later, the music transitioned into the one she would be walking down the aisle to. Uncle Luke appeared at the door the minute she stepped out.

"You look very beautiful, dear," Luke smiled warmly down at her.

"Thanks, Uncle Luke," she smiled.

"You ready?"

She nodded her yes, taking the arm he offered and allowing him to lead her down the path now covered walkway. She was already in awe of the setting, from the snow blanketing the grounds to the vintage shadow box Edison lamps lining the path leading up to the beautiful setting. The guests who'd been paying attention to the maid of honor making her way down the aisle to stand with the other bridesmaids turned to look at her when the piano began playing the song they'd chosen for the march.

A smile broke out on her face as she looked at all the smiling faces watching her make her way down the aisle. A tear pooled in the corner of her eye when she saw her grandmother among those staring with a smile. Her heart warmed, and she felt happy that she could have given her this one joyful memory. Her eyes sought out her mother, who stood at the front with her sisters smiling lovingly at her. She mouthed the words, "I love you."

Rory inclined her head in acknowledgment. Her eyes moved from the smiling faces, and she took the time to take in the aesthetics. She wouldn't lie. As much as Jenny was a hard hat, she had pulled off her vision beautifully.

Faux-white birch trees lined the aisle, and the long white carpet that led up to the gazebo was decorated with white chiffon draping at every window. Garlands, white roses, and pinecones were decorating the pillars. Slowly her eyes moved to where her fiancé stood with the priest awaiting her arrival; then, her gaze trailed up from the custom-made white suit he

A Spectacular Event

wore to connect with his eyes that were already trained on her and filled with love and wonder.

A smile graced his lips, and it was all she could do not to bolt down the aisle and jump into his arms. She wished she could quicken her steps, but instead, she had to keep pace with her uncle. Her heart rate increased with each slow step that took her to him.

"You look...wow. You look beautiful, Ro," James stuttered.

"You look beautiful." she returned, earning a chuckle from James, the priest and his best man who were the closest to hear.

"I mean, you look handsome," she fixed.

"Dearly beloved, we are gathered here to witness the union of two hearts that have chosen to love each other..."

Rory stared into James' eyes as the priest dolled on. All she could think was how happy she was as she briefly looked away from James to the sea of smiling faces staring back at her as they sat under the makeshift tent, acres and acres of white fluffy snow surrounding everywhere else.

This was the best day of her life, and she knew that there were more best days to come, surrounded by the people she loved the most and falling deeper and deeper in love with the man she was marrying today.

Coming Next in the Oak Harbor Series

You can pre order: Bittersweet Moments

Other Books by Kimberly

The Archer Inn Series
An Oak Harbor Series
A Yuletide Creek Series

Connect with Kimberly Thomas

Facebook
Newsletter
BookBub

To receive exclusive updates from Kimberly, please sign up to be on her Newsletter!

CLICK HERE TO SUBSCRIBE

Made in the USA
Monee, IL
05 March 2023